STRINGS OF GLASS

SYDNEY RYE MYSTERIES BOOK 4

EMILY KIMELMAN

For my wonderful husband, Sean, who helps me be brave.

At his best, man is the noblest of all animals; separated from law and justice he is the worst.
—Aristotle

The world is a dangerous place to live; not because of the people who are evil, but because of the people who don't do anything about it.
—Albert Einstein

CHAPTER ONE
GOT TO BE STARTING SOMETHING

The road crumbled under my feet as I ran up it. There is no road surface strong enough to resist the pull back to dirt in this climate. In Goa, Mother Nature rules.

Blue touched my thigh with his nose, a gentle tap to remind me he was there. Thick jungle lined our path. This hill had the fewest homes on our route. No neighbors to wave a hello to or children to smile at as they raced by on bikes either too large or too small for them. There was just me, Blue, the burst of vegetation, and this road of rocks. I reached the top of the hill, my thighs and calves burned. Panting, I struggled to keep my pace.

A low growl narrowed my attention onto a black and white street dog in the brush. Ears flat to her head, she curled her lips and showed teeth. Noting the swollen teats hanging low and exposed, I kept moving. "I'm not going to bother you, mama," I said in a steady voice. "We are just passing by."

Blue slowed, and when I patted my thigh for him to catch up he stopped. I turned to look back at him, my senses on high alert. Blue was a mutt the height of a Great Dane with the coat of a wolf and the long snout of a Collie, with one blue eye and one brown. Blue has saved my life more than once so when he stopped, so did I.

I recognized a twitch on his lip and saw the hackles raise off his shoulders and back making him appear even larger. A deep and rumbling growl left his chest. It was answered behind me. There were suddenly three dogs in our path. None as big or strong as Blue but together they looked dangerous.

I'd been warned about this pack. Growing larger by the day, it was led by an aggressive alpha male the color of dirty water. This must be him, I thought, as the largest of the three, his head wide, fur the silt brown of an engorged river, growled at Blue. The compactness of his body spoke of strength and survival. When he barked, the saliva that shot from his mouth caught a ray of sunlight streaming through the thick foliage around us.

The alpha stepped forward, revving his growl like a teenager on a motorbike. The bitch in the brush flanked our left side and when I turned right, two young dogs, their ears still soft from puppyhood, glowered at me.

The owner of the guest house where I lived warned me to take a stick if I planned on running. "Just in case," she'd said with a dip of her head and a flip of her hand. Because of her advice I carried a light but solid piece of bamboo about twice the thickness of my thumb. I tapped it on the ground in front of me as I backed toward Blue, keeping my eyes forward, focused on the alpha but paying close attention to my peripheral vision, watching the dogs to my sides.

When I reached Blue he moved backwards with me, slowly and deliberately. But the dogs followed. We stopped, and raising the stick over my head, I brought it down hard onto a rock. The loud sound and sudden movement spooked the pups to my right, but the alpha male just growled louder.

The two dogs flanking him went crazy barking, the force of their calls lifting their front paws off the ground. The mother and the young ones joined in raising a ruckus that certainly beat mine. Blue, his front paws planted on the road, exposed his teeth and growled, his pitch wavering up and down. He wanted me to tell him it was okay to attack. I could feel his energy bundling up inside him, roiling around.

Soon I'd have no control.

The alpha charged us, the other two with him following close behind. They weren't coming for me, all they wanted was Blue. It took only an instant for them to cross the space between us. I dropped my stick hard onto the alpha's neck but he ignored my blow, launching himself onto Blue.

Heart pounding I beat at the dogs as they swarmed. The dogs were going for his neck, for the kill. The Mother started to come out of the woods to join in the attack but a quick whack near her with my stick and she retreated into the trees. It only took a glare at the young ones to cow them into keeping their distance.

Blue was holding his own, but bloody streaks marked all the canines. I kicked one of the street dogs hard in the stomach. It fell on its side and then turned on me, ready to fight. I kept it at the end of my stick. It was missing part of one of its ears. A scar across its muzzle looked fresh and pink. Puncture holes in its neck showed where Blue managed a bite. I didn't want to hurt this dog.

I heard a cry and glancing over saw Blue had the alpha on his back. The other dog backed off. The noises they made were not like anything I'd heard before, almost like a speaker that's been turned on its side, spewing squeaks and squeals of interference. The alpha struggled, kicking his legs in the air, trying to push Blue. But he shook his head hard, knocking the dog under him into submission.

The dog at the end of my stick barked at Blue but didn't move toward him. Blue shook his head again and the alpha male yelped. Blood pooled around Blue's lips. "Okay," I said, clapping my hands and getting the rest of the pack's attention. I shooed at them. "Get!" I yelled.

They shuffled away from me.

I stepped forward aggressively, my chest out. "Go!" I commanded. The dog missing part of his ear jumped out of the road and into the jungle, avoiding putting weight onto his left hindquarter. I stepped to the other who growled at me. I pushed him with my stick and he turned on it, biting through the wood. "Hey!" I yelled, pushing it into his mouth hard. He yelped and stepped back. I came at him and he quickly followed the other dog into the trees.

They watched from a safe distance. Blue wasn't letting go of the alpha and I feared that he would kill him. "Blue," I said. He didn't move, just continued to snarl with his mouth full of Silt's soft neck. "Let's go." He flicked his eyes up to my face. A gash on his neck pumped blood. "Come on," I said, making eye contact.

A feral animal looked back at me. There was fear in those eyes, instinct and triumph. The road, I realized, wasn't the only thing that Mother Nature turned to dust here in Goa

CHAPTER TWO
SUTURES AND STITCHES

Blue wasn't limping, but he looked terrible, covered in puncture wounds and a couple of nasty gashes. He appeared to feel no pain though. Walking next to me he stood tall, head high, hackles still a little puffed. Monica screamed when she saw us. "Dilip!" she yelled. "Dilip!" Her driver came rushing around the side of the old Portuguese-style Goan home.

"What happened?" Monica asked, opening the gate for us.

"We got into it with that pack."

Monica gasped. "Are you okay?"

"We need to get him to the vet," I said.

"Of course. Dilip!"

"Yes Madame," he said, standing right beside her. She turned and seeing him there said, "Good, good. Quickly, you must take them to the vet."

She turned to the house and passed Dan, my boyfriend, as she hurried inside. Dan squinted against the bright sunshine. His dirty blond hair was sticking out in the back and his bangs flopped into his pale green eyes. "What's going on?" he asked, his voice still scratchy from sleep. As his eyes focused first on me and then Blue, they widened. "Oh my God, are you okay?" His brow furrowed with concern.

"I'm fine, but Blue..."

"Jesus," he said, taking in the extent of Blue's wounds. "Doesn't look like he went down though."

"No," I said. "How'd you know?"

"The dust, it's only on his legs." Dan was referring to the golden-orange dust that clung to everything in Goa. It was Monica's constant struggle to keep white's white. "How's the other guy look?"

"Not good," I said. "I'm afraid he might die."

"Was it the alpha with that large pack?"

"Yeah." I shook my head trying to free it of the memory of the dog laying on the ground as we walked away, its paws twitching slightly.

Tires crunched and Dilip pulled around front in the guest house's SUV. Monica came out of the house and, opening the back door, motioned for me to get in, a frantic look on her face.

Blue sat next to me in the backseat, his head grazing the roof of the car. He tried to lie down but cried softly, looking to me as he sat back up. "Okay, boy," I said, reaching out a hand to cup his face. He leaned into my palm, resting his good shoulder against the back of the seat. He maintained eye contact. His blue eye, the color of the sky at dusk, and his brown, the color of light passing through a muddy pond, held my grey-eyed gaze.

We drove over a speed bump, bouncing all of us hard. Blue whined and raised a paw scratching at my forearm. I rubbed his face and leaned toward him. "That's okay, you're a good boy. Yes, a very good boy," I whispered.

"Here," Dilip said, passing me a packet of disinfectant wipes. Then he quickly brought his hand back to the gear shift as a moped stopped short in front of us. Dilip swerved into the oncoming traffic lane to pass, narrowly missing a rickshaw.

I took out one of the alcohol soaked tissues and started on Blue's leg. There were some minor scratches crusted in blood and dust on his paw. Holding it gently I placed the tissue against his wounds. Blue licked my hand and whimpered. "Shhh, I have to, shhh," I said.

I moved to a scratch on his nose, holding under his chin. He closed his eyes and let me wipe away the crumbs of dirt. A shiver ran through me as I passed from puncture to puncture on his neck, many of them still gooey with drying blood. Three rags in, Dilip announced we were there.

He swerved onto a sidewalk. "This isn't legal parking," he said as pedestrians poured around us. "So you get out, I'll park and meet you. That's the office right there." Dilip pointed to the dusty building we were stopped in front of.

Dan, Blue, and I walked into a small room that the three of us quickly filled. An unoccupied plastic table and chair took up a quarter of the space. On it, paperwork splayed next to a mess of pens, one of which had leaked ink smearing some of the pages. There were two more doors that lead further into the building.

The whining of a dog floated from another room. Blue sat, scooting close to me, his body tense, his nostrils opening and closing taking in the variety of smells. Dan wrinkled his nose. The strong scent of anti-septic overwhelmed any other odors.

An Indian woman wearing a lab coat over a bright green Kurta came through one of the doors and stopped short when she saw us. "Hello," I said. "We need some help."

Recovering from her initial shock, the woman walked over to the table, casting a cursory glance at Blue. "Fighting?" she asked, shuffling the mess of papers.

"He was attacked," I said.

She nodded absently. "Okay, come through." She pointed to the door next to me and then disappeared back through another behind her. Dan opened the door and we stepped into a long, narrow room completely tiled.

A low bench ran along all the walls, animals in different phases of illness lay on it. A florescent tube on one wall bathed the scene in sterile white light. As we entered, a boxer-looking dog, his hips exposed from malnutrition, lifted his thick head. An IV bag hung above him, a tube snaking down into his leg. A small bitch lay opposite him, fast asleep, the stitches from her recent hysterectomy red, pink, and hideous in the stark light.

Blue reached his neck out to sniff at a puppy who lay curled in a ball, snoring softly. "Blue," I said, pulling his attention to me.

The woman in the lab coat entered through another door pushing a tray with suture instruments clanking on it. "Sit," she said, pointing to an opening on the bench next to the boxer. None of us moved.

I held my hand out. "I'm Sydney," I said. "This is Blue."

The woman nodded. "Lakshmi," she said and then handed me a muzzle. "Put it on him."

Blue looked up at me with trusting eyes as I pushed the cloth onto his snout and clasped it in the back. When I looked up Lakshmi was holding a syringe; she depressed the lever and a small spurt of liquid escaped out.

With gloved hands she inspected Blue's body, occasionally turning to her table and making notes, pushing the needle in at intervals to numb the pain around the worst of his cuts. "The puncture wounds we will leave so that they may drain," she said. "But these lacerations, we have to stitch. And I will need to shave around all the wounds." Lakshmi paused as she came upon the scar on Blue's shoulder.

"From a bullet," I told her. "He saved my life."

She looked up at me from where she crouched next to Blue. "You both like to fight," she gestured toward the scars on my face.

"We seem to bring it out in people."

She clucked her tongue and turned back to Blue's wounds. He whimpered when she touched one. "This is very deep," she said. "You must watch it closely, he must not have too much activities for some time."

Reaching over to her trolley she picked up an electric shaver. Lakshmi plugged it into the wall and when the whirling sound started Blue leaned away from her. "It's okay, boy," I said crouching down next to him. He held my gaze as she reached out and began to cut his coat.

I looked up and saw a smile cross Dan's face. "What's funny?" I asked.

"Nothing," he shook his head.

"No, what?"

"It's just," Dan sighed. "Sorry, but he's going to look ridiculous with patches all over him."

"And that's funny?" I asked. "It's funny that Blue's been hurt?"

Dan's face paled. "Of course not, are you crazy?" Blue whimpered and I placed my hand on the top of his head trying to calm him. "It's just he's such a great looking guy. He's going to look silly."

I shot a glare up at Dan.

"I'm going to stop talking now," he said.

It took forty-five minutes for Lakshmi to finish cleaning up Blue. When done, she peeled off the rubber gloves and dropped them on the tray next to her bloody tools. "He will need antibiotics."

"Okay," I said.

Lakshmi pushed the trolley back toward the entrance she'd used. "Meet me in the front."

We walked back out the door into the small entry room. Dan opened the door to let in some fresh air, with it came the heat of midday.

We stood in silence waiting for the doctor. Blue sat at my feet and let his tongue roll out of his head. I looked down at him, his beautiful coat was interrupted by shaved patches that left his pink skin exposed. The puncture wounds looked tiny and insignificant. One large slash on his neck, now held together by fifteen tiny, black stitches, made my skin crawl.

"I'm sorry about earlier," Dan said.

But as I looked down at Blue, his tongue pulsing with each pant, one back leg kicked out, the shaved spots dotting his once majestic coat I realized he did look kind of silly. I smiled softly and Blue grinned back at me, scooting closer so that he could rest on my foot. "It's okay," I said. "He does look funny. Poor guy."

Lakshmi came back through her door holding a clipboard. She pulled a piece of paper off of it. "Here are the antibiotics that you need and a cream that will help the wounds heal faster. I assume he is up to date on rabies?"

"Yes, he had everything before we came."

"When did you arrive in India?"

"Three months ago."

"Ah, so just at the end of Monsoon," she smiled for the first time since we'd met.

I nodded. "Yes, it was beautiful."

"But very wet," Lakshmi said and then laughed. The sound filled the small space and Dan joined her.

I smiled remembering the moisture that soaked into all of our clothes making it impossible to ever feel dry. "Yes, very damp," I said.

"The most beautiful time though, so green."

"Yes, I love it," Dan said.

"You've come to India before?"

Dan nodded. "This is my fourth visit."

Lakshmi clucked her tongue approvingly. "Very good," she said.

Looking at the clipboard in Lakshmi's hand I asked, "How much do we owe you?" As the question crossed my lips I realized I didn't have my wallet with me.

After making a few notations on the paperwork in front of her Lakshmi handed over the bill. It wasn't much but more than nothing. Dan took it out of my hand. "I've got it," he said.

"Thanks, I forgot my wallet."

Dan smiled. "I know. Where would you keep it in that outfit?"

I looked down at my jogging clothes. I wore light-weight shorts, a sports bra, and a loose tank top. "Yeah, maybe in my shoe," I said with a smile.

Dan handed Lakshmi a pile of rupees. "Remember," she said. "Not so much activity for at least two weeks. Then you bring him back and I check. If you see any infection, come back."

"Thank you," I said.

She shook her head and without another word disappeared through her doorway.

CHAPTER THREE
ON IT GOES

Lunch was waiting when we returned from the vet. Blue leaped out of the car and Monica came running from the house. "Oh, what a poor dear!" she yelled. Her dog, a small street mutt the color of caramel named Lulu, came racing around her. Lulu, her ears pinned to her fox-shaped head, ran right up to Blue and licked at his face. He took the greeting with grace.

Lulu then sat and quickly flipped onto her back. Blue leaned over and nuzzled her. She laid still, her head tilted to the side. Monica reached us then, her lips quivering. "Is he okay?"

"Yes," I said. "We need to get some antibiotics though." Dan pulled the list out of his pocket.

"Oh, Dilip can do that. Dilip!"

"Yes, Madame," he said, standing right beside her.

"Oh, good. Dilip, you must go and get these antibiotics." She motioned at Dan to hand over the list, she then passed it to Dilip who just smiled and nodded. Dan gave him some money and Dilip headed back to the car. "Lunch is ready, come inside," Monica said. "Lulu!" At her name, the small dog jumped back to her feet and raced toward the house.

"You two head to the veranda, I'll just let them know you are ready. Everyone else has eaten."

"I'd like to change first actually, and shower," I said.

"Oh, of course, of course. A half hour?" I nodded. "Good, I'll tell them a half hour."

Dan, Blue, and I walked past the house and followed a stone path through sparsely planted palm trees toward our cabana. There were only five on the property, and on this Tuesday in December they were all full.

Ours was the most secluded, furthest from the pool and the main house. Blue jogged ahead of me reaching the door before we did.

Our cabin had a vaulted ceiling with a fan hanging from it that thumped when it was turned up too high. A king-sized bed with white sheets that were changed every week by the maid, Badlu, was centered in the room. She also cleaned our bathroom, which was maybe my favorite part of the hut. It had an open roof and a Jasmine plant that hung over the wall, filling the space with its floral scent.

Blue went straight to his corner next to the dresser. From that vantage point he could see the front door, but anyone walking in couldn't necessarily see him. Blue circled twice, nosing at the towel he kept there and then lowered onto it with a sigh. "Poor guy is tired," Dan said.

"Yeah," I said. I watched Blue close his eyes and breathe steadily and felt a pang in my chest. I never worried about Blue, he was my rock, the one constant in my life; the only thing I couldn't live without, so I didn't think it was possible for him to go anywhere. But as I stood there in my dirty jogging clothes looking down at his patchy coat and his restful repose, I realized that he wouldn't always be by my side. Blue would die, just like everything else in this impermanent world.

Dan came and wrapped an arm around me. He kissed my forehead. "You okay, hon?"

I leaned against him appreciating his hard chest and strong arms. "Yeah," I said.

"Go on then, hop in the shower," he said, giving my butt a playful slap.

I closed the bathroom door behind me and then turned on the

shower, peeling off my clothing and dropping it on the wood slat floor. The scent of jasmine hung in the humid air, enveloping me into its sweet embrace. Leaning my head back under the spray, my ears filled with the thundering of the hot water on my skull. It was a brief and satisfying moment alone.

My hand trembled slightly as I reached for the shampoo bottle. Exhaling, I stilled my extremities.

Not fear, not rage, excitement. I was excited.

"Dan," I called.

He poked his head in. "Yeah?"

"Join me?"

Dan was not the kind of man you had to ask twice to get in the shower with you. He was kind of always waiting to get in the shower with you. Basically, it was his favorite way to spend time.

It felt good to feel his skin against mine. To press against him, to know that he and I were both real, living, breathing, sentient beings. Not everything is for survival.

EK

Dan left me to get dressed, and I used the edge of my towel to clear the mirror. The steam curled around me clinging back to the cool surface, fogging my reflection. But I knew what was there.

The scars that mar my face pucker a darker pink than the line of damage that slices the outside of my left thigh. My grey eyes shined almost lavender in the light that filtered through the jasmine vine. I pushed my wet hair, dyed with henna to a rich copper, away from my face, raking my fingers through it.

Dan says I have a magnetism about me, but most of the time I'm not really seen. Hugh Defry, my brother's boyfriend at the time of his murder, taught me how to hide. Hugh explained that people only see what they want to see. So I've made myself into something most people don't want to acknowledge exists. Something dark, different and wild. I guess that's magnetic to a few.

My former self, Joy Humbolt, was weak. She got her brother killed and failed to avenge him. Joy ended up a fugitive for a crime she didn't commit. I sighed and turned away from the mirror, not wanting to think about any of it. Not who I was, who I'd been, or who I'd become. Just let me be in this moment, I thought, as I stepped into my cut-off jean shorts and slipped on a T-shirt.

Clean, my hair still damp, Dan and I walked back toward the main house for lunch. Blue stayed on his towel, a bowl of fresh water by his side.

The large, shaded veranda faced the pool, which glittered in the midday sun. A Swedish couple who had arrived two days prior lay on towels next to it, their white-blond hair contrasting with the bright red of their skin. "Why they do that to themselves, I'll never understand," Monica said, looking at the pair. "So many carrots..." she clucked her tongue and went inside to grab us two beers.

Past the pool a river meandered by the property. Occasionally kayakers would pass and local fisherman would row by in their wooden canoes. Monica said it was safe to swim, but Dan heard rumors of crocodiles lurking in the waterways and asked me to stick to the pool, which I did.

Monica returned with our beers and then left us to get the food. The first sip of beer tingled on my tongue, refreshing and bitter, I sighed with pleasure. Dan laughed. "That good, huh?"

I laughed, too. "I guess I'm just thirsty."

Monica returned with a tray of chicken curry, rice, chapati, pickled beets, a salad, and a bottle of water. While I'd had the chicken curry many times, today it seemed richer, spicier, just plain better. I licked it off my fingers and, pulling another chapati from the steaming platter, dug in for seconds. Looking around the glints of sunlight reflecting off the water, the deep blue of the sky, the way the palm trees swayed in the breeze, it all seemed more beautiful, more alive.

It was the fight I realized, the rush of adrenaline. There is nothing like facing mortal danger to make you remember how fucking awesome it is to be alive.

EK

After lunch we went back to the room and I laid down on the bed holding my belly. "Too full," I said.

Dan smiled at me. "You did eat a lot today."

Rolling onto my side I looked over at the small desk in the corner where Dan was fiddling with his computer. He was a computer expert, an absolute genius. That's how we met, I was looking for a programmer who could hack into some email accounts. And he was looking to have an adventure.

"Can I check my email?" I asked.

"Sure," Dan brought me the computer and deposited it on the bed next to me. "I'm going to take a swim."

"Okay, I'll join you in a bit."

I watched as he changed into his suit, enjoying the view of his tight butt and strong back. Blue raised his head when Dan went to leave but quickly fell back to sleep. I climbed off the bed and went over to Blue, peering down at his new stitches. They didn't seem any redder or angrier then when I'd left him.

Returning to the computer I saw that Dan had opened my email for me. I scanned it, hoping to see something from Mulberry. It'd been over a week since he'd contacted me. We'd last seen each other at an airport in Mexico City four months earlier. He'd written almost every day. In the last two months they'd been mostly pleas for me to come back and work with him again. I stopped responding to those emails after the first one when I told him I'd rather die than work for Bobby Maxim, the man who owned Fortress Global Investigations, where Mulberry was a partner. FGI was a powerful and shady private investigation firm that I wanted to stay as far away from as possible. But Mulberry kept writing emails, trying to tempt me with interesting cases. And I kept reading them.

After the fight with those dogs I felt something inside me quivering, waking up, hoping to get out. I closed my email, disappointed that Mulberry hadn't written and disappointed in myself that I wanted him to.

I almost shut the laptop, but one of the tabs on Dan's internet browser grabbed my attention. I clicked on it and my suspicion was confirmed. Dan was on the website about Joy Humbolt, my birth name, the identity I had to give up when I fled the United States after trying to avenge my brother's murder. I escaped New York with stolen treasure, Mulberry, and Blue. In my wake, a legend was born; one that stood for justice and right.

A website was set up where people gathered to talk about their frustrations in facing injustices, pining for the strength of Joy Humbolt. And while I'd met Dan through the site, he knew that I hated it. I despised that glorified, simplified version of my past. Joy Humbolt was not a goddamn hero. And neither is Sydney Rye. While we'd never discussed his leaving the site, I'd always assumed he had. Joy Humbolt was dead, according to me, and thanks to some help from Bobby Maxim (he owed me so it's not like he was doing me any favors, the prick), the authorities agreed. So why was Dan still on this site? I felt anger in my chest, indignation flushed my cheeks. But before I started snooping, I took a deep breath.

The fact was that Dan asked nothing of me. He expected nothing more than what each day brought. Who was I to ask more of him, to tell him how to spend his time? If I started pressuring him then he could do the same to me. I liked how we had it. Neither of us owed the other anything. I closed the laptop determined to mind my own business.

EK

That night I woke up to the sound of dogs howling. It started at one end of the block and traveled down, coming closer and closer until Lulu joined in, adding her own high-pitched call to the chorus. I looked over at Blue, his eyes glowing in the darkness. It lasted for a half hour; the wailing, passing from one canine to the next until the final desperate call of one dog silenced them all.

CHAPTER FOUR
NIGHT FIGHTS

I didn't wake up until late in the morning. Sun came in through one of the open windows, baking me in the sheets. Wrapping myself in a light cotton robe, I stepped out into the day. A thermos filled with piping hot chai waited on my veranda for me. I poured myself a cup, and then picking up one of my worn paperbacks, I started for Dan's garden.

I didn't know if Monica and Dan ever discussed his cultivating a nook of the property, but she loved to visit, bringing him fresh lime sodas and settling down in the dirt, pulling weeds, and chatting until some other duty called her away to a different part of her sprawling landscape.

I found Dan there, hunched over his rows of neatly planted vegetables, a hash joint hanging from his lip. Blue lay nearby in the shade of a tree napping lightly. His head rose as I approached and he stood, heading toward me. Dan looked up and smiled at me. "Hey, sleepyhead."

"Hey, green-thumb."

Dan laughed and then sat back on his haunches holding a handful of bright orange cherry tomatoes. "Want one?" he asked, squinting up at me, his hand extended. I picked my way through the plants and plucked one from his palm. It exploded in my mouth, warm and sweet, fresh

ML

from the vine. I wiggled my toes in the dirt, closing my eyes and enjoying the flavor.

I crouched down next to Dan amidst his garden and he passed me the joint. "Tomatoes are really coming in strong now. I think I'll talk to Monica about making a chutney out of a bunch of them or they'll go bad."

Nodding, I smiled, and inhaled the spicy hash. Dan returned to his work and I watched him for a moment. He was bent over, the ridges of his strong back visible through the soft cotton T-shirt he wore. His shoulders bunched and relaxed as he weeded. Looking around at the vegetables that curled and twisted in the garden I let the hash quiet my mind and dull my senses.

Handing back the joint, I crossed through the garden and settled under a tree in the shade. Blue joined me, curling up into a ball with his back pushed against my thigh. I opened my book and proceeded to join Sookie Stackhouse in her world of vampires and Tiger-men as the sun rose higher in the sky.

Occasionally, I would glance up at Dan and wonder at our relationship. He did not feel like a tether. Everyone else in my life pulled me in one direction or another. He was not like the roots that held his plants in place.

Then how could it be that we wanted all the same things and yet I couldn't see a future with him? Was it because I thought it might be too happy? Was I denying myself something out of guilt or was it something else? A quiver in my belly told me to stay away, not to trust this ease between us. It could be torn away, ripped apart, bludgeoned by resentment, death, any number of enemies hunted for this kind of easy. Fear then, is fear what kept me at bay? And I always thought of myself as brave.

EK

Before lunch I applied the antibacterial cream Dilip had brought for Blue's wounds. I used a Q-tip and lathered the thick, pearl-colored salve onto all of his gashes, punctures, and stitches. Blue looked at me sorrowfully, whimpering occasionally, and even letting out a low yowl of protest when I lingered on one puncture too long.

Getting Blue to take his antibiotics took two pieces of sausage. He ate the first piece but flung the pill across the veranda and under another guest's table. Dan went and grabbed it for me, managing to make the British couple occupying the table laugh, despite their concerned glances. The woman's eyes, green and large in her pale, small-featured face, seemed to wonder if Dan did any of *that* to us. But, I think, she knew somehow that couldn't be true. A single man could not cause so much trauma.

Blue and I couldn't go jogging, and our second day without a run was harder than the first. Blue's wounds began to itch and only my vigilance and a cone, which made him look even more ridiculous, could keep him from injuring himself further. But I knew how he felt. I wanted to lick at my old wounds, too. It'd been almost four years since my brother James's murder but the wound still felt fresh and raw, like a puncture wound that never drained. And without the distraction of running, I felt its itch.

I doubled my Tai Chi time trying to bring peace to my restless mind, but it failed to soothe me. Since coming to India, I'd kept up my jogging and some strength training but there was no sparring. And I began to feel a deep need for a fight.

The fourth night after the dogs attacked us I woke up from a dream clutching the sheets with the sensation that I was falling. I could still hear the echo of rattling breaths that seemed to fill my head, but I didn't remember what the dream was about.

Blue was awake, sitting in his spot, his eyes glowing green in the darkness. I threw away the covers and slipped out of bed. Dan rolled away without waking. I pulled on a T-shirt and sweat pants then opened the door, breathing in the night's cool air. It hit the sweat on my skin, sending a shiver through me. I rubbed my arms and Blue leaned his weight against me.

The property was quiet. The paths were lit by yellow lights doing their best to penetrate the thick blackness that descends in the jungle on a moonless night. The struggling breaths reverberated through my mind and I recognized them as my brother's, some of his last. The scene came back to me in vivid, saturated colors. The blood pumping out of him, his pale face, the rattle of each exhalation. I needed to do something, and it needed to happen right then.

I jogged down the few steps to the lawn, Blue stayed with me. I wished that my trainer, Merl, was there. He could ease my mind, help me understand what to do with all this need inside of me. Or Mulberry, if only to have someone worth punching, or trying to punch in any case. I dropped to the ground and breathed steadily through twenty pushups before leaping back to my feet. That wasn't going to do it

I hadn't seen Merl in years, but the few months we'd spent together on the shore of the Sea of Cortez changed my life. They gave me insight into how powerful calmness can be. I performed a Sun Style Tai Chi through three times but I still itched.

Blue settled on the grass watching me, hoping that he would get to do something. Casting my eyes around I spotted my bamboo walking stick leaning against the porch. It was splintered at one end where the street dog bit it. Glancing over at our motorcycle parked in the grass I saw a pile of tools. Dan had been working on the old Bullet. Next to the tools, a lead pipe lay discarded in the dirt. I picked it up and spun it in my fingers the way Merl taught me, feeling its weight. One side was heavier than the other. I swung it through the air and it whistled in a way that made my heart beat faster.

I swung it again, dropping a knee to avoid an imaginary attack. Spinning, I lashed out at my fictional opponent. And then I was lost—sucked into the center of my mind where nothing mattered but staying alive. Swift, knowing, calm movements. Nothing wasted. Everything for one purpose. Total concentration and freedom from that nagging, nasty itch.

The half-remembered dream of struggling breaths and the terrifying sensation of plummeting through open space woke me every night for the next seven. And so I rose, and I fought imaginary foes.

Blue's punctures drained and his body began to close the wounds. The skin around his stitches changed from a bright and urgent red to a simple pink. Within two weeks we were back on the road, running, practicing commands, training hard for something or possibly nothing.

In that time the Christmas holiday passed and a new year was born. My body became tighter, the tension building with each nighttime training session. My shape lost all the softness that the months of lazing about had allowed. When I look back on this now, I wonder if my instincts were just so tuned that somehow I knew a fight was coming. Or did all my preparations draw me there? Was it my will or my fate? I still wonder if there is a difference.

CHAPTER FIVE
BLAST FROM THE PAST

Though I'd become practically nocturnal, Dan and I were no more drifting apart than we had drifted together. While I slept, he gardened and spent time on his computer doing I didn't know what. But after three weeks I came back from a two hour run late in the afternoon with mud on my legs and leaves in my hair. I stripped down for my shower and as I headed for the bathroom Dan looked up from his laptop and said, "Hey, can I talk to you about something?"

"Sure," I said.

"I see how that fight affected you."

I shrugged. "Yeah."

"I see the glint in your eye, Sydney. I mean, hell, I love lying around with you and reading books and chilling, but that doesn't mean that you are going to be happy here. Not for long anyway."

I bit my lip not wanting to talk about it. The first time I felt anything like this it was a wild crazy burn. It burned Joy away. But Sydney was made of sterner stuff. Practically made of stone. I could get through this without hurting anyone, I thought.

"My point is I know that you need something to do."

I didn't answer, waiting to see where this was going. Dan sighed and stood up, tilting his computer screen toward me. I saw that it was the Joy Humbolt website and closed my eyes. "Dan—"

"Wait," he said, interrupting me. "Look, it's not the same as it was. It's not so much about Joy anymore." His voice rose as he became more excited. "Now it's about fighting for justice."

I cocked my head at a sarcastic tilt. "Fine, what's it called?"

He swallowed. "Joyful Justice."

"You want me to be involved in something called Joyful Justice. Are you insane?"

He flopped his head. "Come on, Syd—"

"No, really," I laughed. "Seriously, have we been hanging out at all?"

"Yeah, Syd, and you're not some badass vigilante, you read Sookie Stackhouse mysteries."

My jaw dropped. "You recommended them."

"Yeah, and I like Joyful Justice."

"Dan, I don't want to talk about this," I said again.

"I know, babe, I know that but I just wanted to bring it up. I just wanted to plant the seed in your brain." He came and wrapped his arms around my waist. He kissed the top of my head and then leaned back, his arms still linked around me. "But, just so you know, I think Mulberry would agree with me."

"What?" I said. "You've been talking to Mulberry about this?"

He shrugged. "No, I just think he'd agree." An evil little smile played on his lips.

"Don't try to manipulate me, Dan."

His lips straightened. "Manipulate you?" He dropped his arms and turned away.

"Yeah."

He looked over his shoulder at me. "Sometimes you say the most fucked up shit." And with that he walked out the door leaving it open. I watched him as he crossed the lawn to our motor bike. He got on, and with a putter and blast the old Bullet roared to life. Dan pulled out of the drive and onto the road without looking back at me.

His sudden anger was totally out of character. I was the one who got all crazy and he was the one who stayed totally calm. I looked around the little hut at Dan's T-shirts in a neat pile on top of the dresser. My flip flops askew by the door. His bug spray, sunscreen, and hand sanitizer neatly lined up on his side of the bed. All there was on my side was a pile of paperbacks, old and fat from the tropics. I used his sunscreen and bug spray. He read my pile of books. We were living together. I was living with a man. A man named Dan. I swallowed, oh shit, we had roles, we were in a god damn relationship. And that was our first fight. Shit.

I was already in my towel ready for my shower so I decided to take it. Stepping into the bathroom I inhaled the rich scent of jasmine. A lizard dashed up the wall and into the vine's fragrant flowers.

The water sputtered for a moment and then streamed hot and heavy. Stepping under the spray I closed my eyes and concentrated on getting clean. I heard Blue barking excitedly and wondered if Dan had come back. Were we going to make up now? I remembered how fun that could be and thought that maybe I could do this relationship thing again. Maybe I was ready. My heart fluttered at the thought.

EK

Finishing quickly I dried off and headed back into the hut. Throwing my towel on the bed I reached for a sundress when a voice behind me said. "Whoa, whoa."

I turned around to see Mulberry sitting in my reading chair, his left hand covering his eyes. I grabbed the towel off the bed and when I turned back he was peeking. "Mulberry!" I yelled.

He shrugged and dropped his hand. "What?"

"Jesus, what are you doing here?" My heart was pounding in my chest.

"When you refused to respond to my emails I figured I'd show up."

I rolled my eyes even though I was really happy to see him. If I was wearing more clothes and he'd actually knocked, I would have hugged him. Blue sat next to him leaning into his legs. Mulberry reached out and ruffled his ears.

"Why have you been ignoring me?" he asked, looking at me with his bright green eyes.

I sighed. "Why do you insist on only writing to me about cases?"

Mulberry smiled. "Because I know a good mystery is the best way to your heart; isn't that right, Blue?" Mulberry said, returning his attention to my beast. Blue looked up at him, his eyes filled with devotion and joy. "At least he's happy to see me," Mulberry said. "What happened to him? I'd hate to see the other guy," he said with a soft laugh.

"He was attacked by an aggressive pack. And I would be happy to see you, if *you* hadn't just seen me naked."

Mulberry laughed. "Come on, what are you doing here?"

"What do you mean? I'm living here."

"I can see that," he said, then looked around the cabin. I saw his jaw clench and then he asked quietly, "With Dan?"

"Yes, with Dan."

"And that's what you want to do?" He looked over at me again, glints of yellow in his eyes sparkled in the sunlight that streamed through a nearby window.

"What do you mean?"

"You want to stay here, not have any more adventures with me?"

"Your *adventures* usually involve Bobby Maxim, lies, and almost getting me killed," I said.

Mulberry frowned. "What are you going to do?" He stood up and stepped toward me, his broad shoulders blocking out the sun's rays. "Stay here and marry Dan? Become a homemaker?" I felt anger rolling off of him like a wave of heat surges over blacktop in the desert.

His rage struck me like an unexpected blow, and I yelled at him. "Why not, Mulberry? Why wouldn't I marry Dan? Because that might make me happy? Shouldn't I be happy!"

His face paled and he shrunk away from me. I felt like a bull, huffing air out my nose, ready to charge. He shook his head. "I'm sorry, Sydney. Of course you should be happy." The word seemed to die in his mouth. He ran a hand through his dark hair, the silver that peppered it shining in the light.

I squeezed my eyes shut and rubbed at them with my free hand. "God Mulberry, what are you doing here?"

"I don't know," he said, not looking at me. A moment passed as we stood there, the steam from my shower and heat of our emotions filling the room with a wet and heavy silence. Mulberry licked his lips. "I'm sorry."

I nodded, my damp hair tickling my bare shoulders. "Want a drink?" I asked.

He smiled. "Yeah, I'd like that."

"All right, then get the fuck out so I can get dressed." I smiled at him.

Mulberry laughed and turned to the door, Blue following him outside.

When I came out Mulberry was sitting by the pool with Monica. She laughed and placed her hand on his forearm as he leaned toward her. When I walked up to them Monica was blushing. "Oh, Sydney," she said. "Your friend is so charming." Mulberry smiled up at me, squinting against the sun behind me.

"Really?" I said. "Not usually."

Ignoring me Monica said, "I'll send Badlu out with some drinks for you. What would you like?"

"Two tequila gimlets with a splash of cran," Mulberry answered.

"You two must know each other well," Monica said.

"Yes," Mulberry said, not taking his eyes off me. "We go back a long time."

Monica laughed again, and I saw her resist touching his broad shoulder. Mulberry looked good. He'd lost the weight I'd last seen him carrying around. Those boulder arms were back, the same ones he had when I first met him in New York, a full-on lifetime ago. "You look good," I said as I sat next to him. "Back in shape."

Mulberry smiled. "Nothing like a near-death experience to make you remember you want to live."

I nodded but didn't say anything, scared by how the man was saying my thoughts out loud. Maybe he'd always done that and I'd just never noticed. "It's hot out here, huh?" Mulberry said.

"The sun will be down soon."

"Come on," he stood up and pulled me out of my chair. "Let's sit with our legs in the pool."

I laughed. "You're kind of like a kid."

"Only when I'm around you."

He rolled up his khakis and I sat on the tiled edge, slipping my calves into the cool water, pulling my dress up to my thighs. Mulberry settled next to me, close enough that our hips almost touched. Badlu came out with our drinks and Mulberry held up his glass to mine. "To happiness," he said.

I clinked my glass, brimming with light ruby liquid, against his. A little splashed as our glasses touched. Mulberry reached down and sucked it off his hand. I watched as the sunlight caught the saliva on his lips making them sparkle in the final rays of the day.

"Are you happy, Mulberry?" I asked.

He looked up at me and the glints of yellow in his green eyes twinkled. "Enough," he said. "I'd be happier if you—" He cut himself off and shook his head. "I'm happy that you're happy."

I turned away from his penetrating gaze looking out onto the river that meandered by. Two fishermen rowing with strong strokes propelled their wooden canoe through the muddy water. One of them said something and the other laughed. The sound carried across the water like an echo.

"I miss you sometimes," I said.

Mulberry wrapped his arm around my back. "I miss you, too."

We sat like that, sipping our drinks, his heavy arm hugging me close. I leaned into his chest smelling a man I realized I knew so well. Mulberry saved my life in more than a physical sense. The man pulled me out of my misery, my denial, and my loathing; he always came and got me when I needed him to. Did he need me now? Was I missing a call for help? Or was it the other way around?

The sun set behind us and the stars began to pop out of the pale blue sky. Our glasses sat empty by our sides and we didn't talk. Blue came and curled up at our backs, resting against us. There didn't seem to be anything to say. We shared a past filled with violence and triumph, strong emotions and death. Is this what kinship meant? I wondered.

"I should get going," Mulberry said, breaking into my thoughts.

I nodded turning my face into his chest, pressing my eyes so hard that spots exploded in my vision. I loved it here, squeezing against him. It felt like a kind of home, a safe place.

Mulberry turned and brushed his lips against my hair. A thrill ran down my spine, something I'd never felt with him before. He kissed my forehead and reached a hand up, stroking the back of my neck. Heat rose to my cheeks and I pulled away looking up at him. Mulberry stared out into the darkening sky, his jaw clenching. I watched the muscle jump and thought about reaching up and kissing it. Shocked by the thought I dipped my head onto his chest again.

Blue stood and I turned to see Dan walking down the path. When he saw me his eyes hardened. Mulberry turned to look. Seeing Dan, he unwrapped his arm from around me. We both stood.

"Hey," Dan said.

"Hey," Mulberry said, his voice gruff. He extended his hand and Dan took it, his chest puffed out, and a scowl on his face. "I was just leaving."

"Yeah?"

Mulberry turned to me and then back to Dan. "You're a lucky man," he said.

Dan seemed to soften. "Why don't you stay for dinner?" He smiled tightly. "I know Monica would love that."

Mulberry laughed. "I'm sure," he said grinning, "but I've got to go."

"A case?"

Mulberry nodded. "I came to try to tempt your lady away to help but she won't have it," he said, looking over at me. I dipped my head looking down at my wet feet, pruney from how long they'd swung in the pool. "Says she's happy," Mulberry continued, turning back to Dan.

Dan just nodded. "I hope so," he said.

"It was good to see you," Mulberry said to Dan. "Mind if I have one more minute with her before I go?"

Dan's jaw tightened but he nodded and walked toward our hut. Blue followed him, tapping his head into Dan's hand, looking for more of a greeting. Mulberry turned to me. "If you ever want to blow shit up or anything call me, okay?"

29

"You know there is no one I would rather die with," I said quietly.

Mulberry smiled softly and then stepping close to me, too close, he reached up and brushed my bangs aside, looking at the scars on my forehead. He leaned down and brushed a kiss onto the pink line that ran along my eyebrow into my hairline. Then ran his thumb along the thicker line that puckers the skin under my left eye. He stepped even closer so that our bodies touched. Tilting my chin up so that he was looking into my eyes he said, "I don't want to die with you, Sydney, but if you ever want to live again..." He leaned in and kissed me on the lips, softly, almost chastely, except for the electric shock that ran between us.

I stepped back and he smiled. I felt that my cheeks were flushed red. Without another word Mulberry turned and walked up the path toward the main house. My heart thumped in my chest. I turned toward our hut and Dan was standing there, a murderous look on his face.

CHAPTER SIX
GETTING INTO IT

I walked up the path towards him, guilt heavy on my shoulders.

"You want to go get some dinner?" I asked Dan.

He was chewing on his lip. "What was that?" he asked, gesturing toward where Mulberry and I just stood.

"What?" I said, walking by him headed up to our cabana. Blue followed me, pushing his head into my hand.

"What? Really?" He followed me. "Are you kidding?"

"We're old friends," I said, not turning to look at him.

"That's not how I say goodbye to my friends."

I climbed the few steps onto our veranda and pushed through the door. Blue ran to his bed and picked up a bone Monica had brought him from the market. He pranced over to me displaying his prize.

"Come on, Dan, there is nothing between me and Mulberry, we've just been through a lot together," I said, hoping that was the truth but suddenly unsure.

"That didn't look like nothing," Dan said, his voice a low rumble. "That looked like he kissed you."

"Hardly," I said, pulling my dress over my head.

"Then how come your cheeks are red? You think I can't tell what's going on with you?"

I sighed as I pulled jeans out of my dresser. "Come on, let's just go get some dinner, okay?"

"No, it's not okay!"

I turned to look at him, a tank top in my hand, my jeans unbuttoned. "You're acting a little out of control," I said.

Dan stepped up to me. "I don't ask much of you Sydney, do I?"

"What?"

"Have I asked much of you, anything at all really?"

"No," I said.

He was standing right in front of me, using his size to try to intimidate me. Dan must be really mad, I thought, because he was making mistakes.

"All I want is for you to just fuck one guy at a time."

I looked up into his grape-green eyes, they were narrow slits staring down at me. I almost punched him, the anger in my chest balled my fists, but even through his jealousy and rage I could see pain in his eyes. That kiss hurt him. I didn't need to hit him to hurt him. I'd already done it.

"You don't ask for anything because I never offered anything," I said quietly, my voice the texture of cool stone. "You want to be with me, get used to getting hurt. That's what you get with me. Pain."

I shrugged into my tank top and, grabbing my leather jacket from the closet, started toward the door. Blue followed me, falling into line with my hip, sensing my mood.

"Sydney, wait," Dan said, following me out into the night.

I kept walking steadily toward our bike. I needed the speed, the freedom, I needed to get the fuck away from this mess.

He grabbed for my hand and I whirled around on him. Blue let out a growl of warning. "I'm not some girl, some prize, some whatever. You don't own me. I'm not a bitch," I said through clenched teeth.

"I'm sorry."

"Yeah, me too," I said, turning away. He let me walk to the bike alone. Blue barked at me when I climbed aboard. "Stay here, boy," I said. "I'll be home later." Grabbing the handles I kicked at the crank once, twice, and the third time she roared to life. I revved the engine feeling the power of the machine between my legs, then letting go of the clutch sped out onto the road.

EK

The night enveloped me, splintered by florescent tube lights angled on poles that lit up the green foliage like a movie shoot. The whoosh of wind in my ears blocked out all other sounds except for the rumble of the Bullet's engine and the crunch of her tires on the rough road. I steered through the village. My headlights caught the reflective green eyes of a stray dog picking through garbage on the side of the road. A cow meandered out of the darkness causing me to swerve around it, my heart in my throat. I slowed down, easing back on the gas. A tightness in my chest rushed me forward though. I didn't know where I was going, but I knew I wanted to get there fast.

Through the rural village out into the open space of the fields, I rode past neatly lined crops lit by a big moon that hung like a gaping smile in the dark sky. A fire blazed on the side of the road, and I flew through its smoke breathing in the acrid scent of burning plastic. Three men watched me pass, their only movement the swivel of their heads as I flew by.

I hit the highway picking up speed, maneuvering around trucks, tall and off- balance looking. "Please" "Horn" "Okay" written across their wide rears encouraging other drivers to announce their presence with a toot. Which they did in a constant chorus, like the croaking of frogs on a summer night. Two men on a scooter, both chatting on their cell phones, smiled at me as we sped by each other, only inches separating our bikes. A taxi with only one headlight blinded me, swerving into my lane around a truck holding cases filled with live chickens that squawked their fright into the night. I honked my horn, skidding around the cab, its driver, hunched, old, and unworried.

The town of Mopsa slowed me down, congestion clogging its tiny roads, unprepared for the mighty nation they now supported. Giant buses idled in a row blocking traffic. The drivers yelled, waving their arms, and shaking their heads at each other and the customers who lined up to board. Thin men, languid in their movements, walked in groups, their arms slung around each other. Women, wearing the colors of tropical birds, their heads down, slipped through the congestion. I pushed through, easing my way between the tight spaces that the city left me. Fitting myself in.

One last traffic circle and I made it back onto the open road, hurtling toward the sea. The scent of the Arabian Sea filled my nostrils before I realized where I'd driven myself. A deserted beach Dan and I liked to go to. Just one bar, a few old and rusty sun beds. I stopped the Bullet, cut the engine, and listened to the thundering of the waves against the shore.

Pulling the Bullet onto her kickstand I walked toward the beach, slipping off my shoes and letting my toes feel the cool sand between them. A grove of palm trees skirted the beach. I sat next to one, leaning my back against its solid trunk. The wind whistled through the palms above my head. Not far a coconut fell to the ground with a solid, dangerous thunk.

I stared out at the sea, brown and rough, with white foam spilling off the top of each wave as it crashed into a frothy mess, rushing up the sand then back again, comforting in its violence and consistency. I thought about the gentle caress of Mulberry's lips and reached up to touch my own, wondering what I felt. I'd never experienced that between us before. Comfort, camaraderie, friendship, yes, all those things but never electricity. With Dan, I felt sizzling between us from the moment we met. I'd thought he understood me, what I was capable of giving. But it was my fault really, I forgot to keep him at arm's length; I let him feel safe with me, like I was a person you could love and live with.

Mulberry knew that wasn't true. He knew me and how dangerous I was. Maybe I'd underestimated how dangerous he might be to me.

Voices distracted me from my thoughts.

CHAPTER SEVEN
THE FIGHT IN THE DOG

Men's voices floated through the trees; laughter that sounded mean, I thought. Then I heard the muffled cries of a woman. The hairs on the back of my neck spiked. A scream ripped through the air and I jumped up. Slipping back into my shoes I moved toward the sounds—men laughing, a woman crying.

At the end of the grove of trees the beach opened up. Inland was a garbage-strewn parking lot used during the day by beach-goers. The sounds were coming from there. I peeked around a tree and saw a van and several scooters. The headlights of the van backlit a group of maybe six or seven guys. A figure broke free and stumbled toward the sea.

The men laughed and one ran after her. Hidden in the trees I held my breath. Their laughter sounded like the cackles of a pack of hyenas feasting on carrion.

The woman struggled through the sand, her body jerking violently as she ran desperately away. Long black hair flowed out behind her, a thigh-length kurta hung in tatters off her shoulders, one breast exposed, swinging in the moonlight. When the man, young, slight and gangly, caught her she fell forward onto her hands and knees. He kicked her and as she flew onto her back I saw her bare ass.

Looking again at the group that laughed and cheered, I pulled my lead pipe out of the folds of my jacket. I had surprise on my side, but I had a feeling those jackasses would be on me quick. The woman was a fighter, though. She was pushing herself through the sand away from the man as he unbuttoned his pants. I waited until he grabbed her and was down on his knees, trying to control the woman who was sobbing and fighting him off with all her strength before sprinting out onto the beach.

The men up the hill stopped laughing as I crossed into their view. Raising the pipe behind me I brought it up sure and quick onto the kid's chin, following through so that his blood sprayed in an arc out into the night. Not even waiting for his body to hit the sand I turned to the woman laying prone on the ground.

I offered her my hand. "We need to go now," I said. She blinked up at me, sand stuck in her eyelashes. Sobs still racked her body, her face wet with tears and swollen from a beating. "Now!" I yelled, seeing the movement of men up the hill. She jumped into action then, grabbing my hand and leaping to her feet. I pulled her behind me sprinting back into the trees as the men closed the distance between us.

She struggled to keep up with me, but I yanked her forward until we reached a small cement shed in the thick of the trees. I pulled her to the far side and rested against the wall, my breathing even.

"Stay here," I said. She grabbed the sleeve of my coat.

"Please," she said, struggling for breath. "Don't leave me." Her eyes were black and huge. Her accent British.

"Stay," I said, slipping back into the trees. There was garbage all over the place. The men stomped through it, crackling on plastic water bottles, and tinging on cans. They were walking around like they were not vulnerable; like they were the lions. Ha!

Crouching, I ran back toward the beach. One of the men, fat and disgusting, his belly hanging exposed under his too-short shirt yelled something, and another man answered laughing. He was about twenty feet into the trees and alone, didn't even have a flashlight. What was his plan, beat me to death with his dick?

I circled around my would-be attacker and then leapt lightly onto his back bringing my pipe across his neck and squeezing. The man smelled like rotten meat and sweat. He brought his chubby hands up and tried to pry the pipe from his throat but quickly dropped to his knees, then onto his face. When his breathing stopped so did the pressure on my pipe. I slid back behind a big tree trunk waiting for the other man they'd sent after us.

He called out once, twice, and by the third time, he'd found his friend laying lifeless. Before the yell of warning could leave his lips I brought the lead pipe hard behind his knees. He grunted as much in surprise as pain, and I stepped forward bringing the pipe across the back of his head. He fell onto the dead man, and I ran back to the woman.

She was huddled against the wall, her torn kurta slit up to expose her bare hips.

"Here, take my pants." I unbuttoned and pulled them down, glad that I wore boy shorts rather than bikinis underneath. I pulled them over my worn low-top Converse sneakers and pushed them at the woman.

She took them with a trembling hand. "Thank you."

"Come on, we need to keep moving. I only got two."

She stepped into the jeans, gingerly pulling them up over her hips. I held my hand out and she took it. I led her quickly back toward my bike. The road continued down to a tourist town. I hoped that we could ride away without them noticing.

But before we even reached the Bullet I heard the whine of the van's engine and the buzzing of several scooters cutting through the night. I climbed onto the motorcycle, and she got on behind me. She wrapped her arms around my waist and clasped her fingers.

I cranked it once, twice, three times, but the Bullet stayed silent. Shit! The van rolled down the road, its high beams reflecting off the beat up chrome of the Bullet and making the night around us seem that much darker. "Come on, baby!" I yelled, jumping onto the crank hard. A putter. "Now!" I jumped again, shaking the bike, willing the damned engine to start.

A scooter shot out past the van, and I made eye contact with the man riding it right as the Bullet backfired with a loud bang and a puff of black smoke. I took a deep breath and stomped on the crank one more time. The engine came alive, vibrating the bike. She was ready to ride.

I peeled out, spraying rocks. The ting of them hitting the scooter told me how close they were. I lowered over my handles; the woman clung to me, pressing her face against my back. The road sloped down sharply and I took it at full speed. My headlight caught a rut in the road just in time for me to choose a bank. The Bullet was faster than the scooter and, checking my mirrors, I saw that I'd gained some distance but there were three scooters and a van following us.

The road turned to pavement and quickly the town surrounded us. Tourists, sunburned and dreadlocked, meandered along the side of the road. They looked frozen in space as I raced by them. The main road was too congested, and I knew they'd be on us in seconds. Taking a chance I turned into one of the narrow alleys lined with shops. Merchants selling sarongs, elephant-patterned bedspreads, and long-strapped bags dotted with mirrors jumped out of my way as I barreled down the alley.

I felt the woman look behind us. "We lost the van," she said.

I turned again and the woman yelled, "No, it's a dead end. Go back!" I didn't hesitate, braking hard and reversing at full speed. When I backed out a scooter was right there. I turned hard and accelerated away but he pulled up alongside us, reaching out for the woman on the back of my bike.

I steadied myself and then concentrating hard, kicked out with my left leg hitting the front of his bike. He flipped, the back tire arching by our heads, and then we raced ahead as the scooter slid behind us on a bed of sparks. We sped out of the town and into the fields.

Two scooters pursued us, one with two guys on it. I took off down a dirt ridge that ran along a culvert which brought water out of the town. The stench of sewage was ripe as we roared through the open space. When we reached the river the woman said, "That way, towards the highway." I turned the bike at the top of the hill, my bare leg glowing in their headlights. On my thigh the thick ridge of a scar from the last time I got shot stood out puckered and pink.

I wanted to send the three guys into the sewage that sulked by but there was no way...unless I got off the bike and faced these ignorant fucks right there. I revved the engine watching their approach.

"What are you doing? We need to go!" the woman said, squeezing me around the belly.

"Do they have guns?" I asked.

"Yes!" she squealed. "Come on." She pushed me. "What are you doing?"

I revved the engine and this time let it catch, sending us shooting along the dirt road past the neatly lined crops. I sped up, headed for the tree line, my engine roaring. We hit a bump and got some air; I felt the breath rock in my lungs, my heart jump in my throat.

We entered the highway at full speed. I let my instincts take over and followed the flow of traffic, feeling my way through its slippery fingers. Honking sounded on all sides of us. I ground my teeth, sick of running. I braked hard, sticking out my foot to steady us as I burned a circle in the road. Smoke billowed behind us as I raced back toward our attackers. I reached into my jacket and pulled out my pipe, keeping it low and out of sight. The first scooter only had the one guy on it. He saw me coming and pulled a gun, sending himself a little off-balance. I flew by him sticking out my pipe as I went, taking the mother fucker off his bike. The impact ricocheted down my arm, shooting pain through my shoulder blade.

His scooter crashed hard, sending his body flying, limp and helpless under the wheels of a truck. My heart raced and I took a deep breath. Darting through the traffic I looked for the other scooter. "Where are they?" I yelled over my shoulder.

"I don't know," the woman cried. "I don't see them."

Fine, I thought, and pulled over. There was gridlock from the "accident" behind us. The woman stayed locked onto me. I scanned the thickening crowd. Scooters were eking by the mess but vans, trucks, and cars lined up behind the spill. Honks rose from the crowd like a Greek chorus.

"Maybe they ran," the woman suggested.

"Yeah," I said. "Do you want to go to the police?" I asked.

"No," she answered.

I pulled back into traffic, maneuvering past the accident. A girl on the back of her father's scooter pointed at me. I put a finger to my lips and her hand dropped by her side, a look of terror on her face. The distant sound of sirens wailed as we pulled by the accident: a smear of slick blood lit by bright white headlights; men standing around with their palms pressed against the small of their backs, heads shaking with regret.

We rode in silence, the Bullet purring under us. I turned off the highway toward my place. She started to cry as we wound through the small roads. Taking one hand off the handles I placed it over hers, clasped on my waist. "You're safe now," I said.

She nodded against my back. "Thank you."

CHAPTER EIGHT
SPLIT AND SWOLLEN

Lulu, her ears pinned to her fox-shaped head, barked as we pulled into the driveway. She ran alongside the bike as I navigated to our cabana. Dan stood on the veranda; warm yellow light pouring from our open door backlit him. Blue barked and trotted over to us, joining Lulu by our side. My heart squeezed at the thought that I was home.

Dan came down the steps following Blue. The woman stayed glued to me even after I turned off the engine. "Come on," I said. "We're here."

She raised her head off my back and looked at Dan who stood next to the bike, his face a mask of concern. "Are you okay?" he asked, as his eyes roamed over my face and down my body.

I nodded. "Yes, we're fine now." I patted the woman's hands. "Come on."

Her fingers slowly unclenched, and she gingerly climbed off the bike. Her legs unsteady, she almost fell but Dan caught her. She recoiled from him, bumping back into me, holding the tatters of her shirt against her chest.

I wrapped an arm around her, just managing to keep the bike up at the same time. Dan quickly grabbed the handles. "I've got it," he said. "Take her inside."

Climbing off the bike with my arm around the woman wasn't easy but I managed. As we walked toward the cabana, Blue fell into an easy heel and Lulu circled us, her ears pinned to her head with excitement. She barked and went to jump on the woman but Blue blocked her with a growl. Lulu immediately backed off, her tail between her legs.

"What's your name?" I asked as we stepped through the open door.

"Anita," she said. Her whole body was shaking as I sat her down on the bed. Dan followed us in and stood by the door offering her some space.

"Get her a glass of whiskey," I said.

Dan complied, pulling the bottle of Kentucky Bourbon out of our closet and pouring the woman a stiff drink. She took it with a hand that shook. "Go on," I said. "Drink it." Dan looked at me and I nodded that yes, I'd like a stiff one, too.

He grabbed another glass off our bureau and poured me two fingers. As he did, our guest drank hers down in gulps. When she lowered the glass there was a fire in her eyes that wasn't there a moment ago.

"Feeling better?" I asked.

She nodded. "Yes, thank you."

"Do you want a shower?"

She looked down at her torn, filthy shirt. "Yes, thank you."

"I've got clothing you can borrow." Dan handed me my drink and I took a big swallow, relishing the whiskey's burn as I moved toward my dresser. When I turned back with a clean towel, underwear, linen pants, and a shirt, the woman's chin was wobbling. "Come on," I said, taking her elbow gently. "You can have a good cry in the shower." Her eyes darted up to mine, brimming with tears and ringed in red. She sniffled. I smiled at her. "It's fine. Come on." She followed me into the bathroom. Placing the towel and clothing on the closed toilet lid, I got the hot water going.

"What's your name?" she asked as I turned to leave.

"Sydney, Sydney Rye."

"Thank you," she said, the words catching in her throat.

"You're welcome. I'll see you outside. Take your time. There's more whiskey when you're ready."

She gave me a brave smile and I left.

Dan sat on our bed, a fresh glass in his hand. "My God," he said. "What happened?"

I sat down next to him. He put a hand on my bare thigh and squeezed. I leaned against him and inhaled. He smelled like sunscreen and sea salt. "She was about to be raped," I said, keeping my eyes shut, staying in the dark rapture of his scent. "I stopped them and we escaped."

Dan wrapped his arm around me and I cuddled closer into his body. "I bet those guys look like shit right now," he said into my hair.

"You know me too well. But I didn't get them all. I lost a van and two guys on a scooter."

"What do you mean 'lost'?"

I just shook my head thinking of the dark figures that chased us through the fields, their faces obscured. Dan kissed my hair.

I heard the shower turn off and sat up. "I should put some pants on."

"Here," Dan leaned across the bed and handed me my sarong.

I looked at it, the simple piece of cloth I'd worn almost every day for the last three months. It was sun-stained, faded, and soft. I shook my head. "I think I need real pants," I said, standing up and heading to my dresser.

"I'll admit I like the look," Dan said behind me. I glanced over my shoulder and he was staring at my ass.

"Dan!"

He looked up at me. "What?" he said with a shrug. "You pull up on that bike without pants on and wearing a leather jacket, what do you want from me?"

I laughed feeling something loosen in my chest as I pulled out a pair of jeans. Slipping into them I said, "I guess that's sweet."

"Damn straight it is," Dan said, standing up. He wrapped his arms around my waist and kissed my forehead. "I'm sorry about earlier."

"Yeah, me too," I said.

"Let's not do that, okay?"

"Do what?"

"Fight, you know, couple stuff. Let's not."

I grinned up at him. "You read my mind."

He leaned in for a kiss, but the squeak of the bathroom door broke his attention from my lips.

Anita stood in the doorway, steam floating around her. Her long black hair was combed straight. My teal blue linen shirt was a little snug but fit her well enough. She'd had to roll the cuffs of my pants and they hung loosely around her hips. Anita held her ruined top and my jeans in her hands. The bruises on her face looked painful and raw.

"Here, I'll take those," I said, stepping around Dan. I dropped the kurta into a plastic bag and put my jeans in the laundry pile.

Dan stepped toward the door, giving Anita as much space as he could in the small hut. Noticing his move, Anita grimaced. "I'm sorry," she said, "for reacting like that."

"Please, I totally understand," Dan smiled at her.

"Sit down," I said. "We need to tend to your face."

Anita smiled painfully. "It does look quite awful, doesn't it?"

"Here," I refilled her glass. "For the pain."

She sat on the bed and sipped at the whiskey.

I got our first aid kit out and rummaged around until I found the things I needed. After dabbing sterile gauze with alcohol I reached out and held Anita's chin lightly, tilting it up into the light. They'd done a real number on her. Anita's left eye was cut at the eyebrow, her nose was swollen, and crusted blood still clung around her nostrils. Her top lip was split open.

"Did you lose any teeth?" I asked.

"No," she said, looking up at me. Her eyes were almond shaped, a brown so rich they looked black, with long eyelashes. When not beat up I bet she looked real pretty.

I cleaned the wounds, she winced against the pain. "Dan," I said, "grab me some of the stuff we've been using on Blue."

Dan moved to the desk and grabbed the bottle of cream, handing it to me. I put a little on a Q-tip and slathered it onto all of her open wounds.

"Ice," I said. Dan went to the mini fridge, and I heard the popping of cubes from their tray. He wrapped them in a washcloth and handed the bundle to me. "Here," I said, placing the pack against her eyebrow first. "Hold this there. Twenty minutes, then we'll move it down to your lips."

She nodded, reached up and held the cloth to her face.

"Did you know those guys?" I asked, stepping back and picking up my glass. Dan refilled it and I leaned against the small desk, kicking my feet out in front of me.

"Not by name," Anita said.

"You're British?" I asked.

She shook her head. "No, but I was educated in England."

"Terrible weather," I said.

She smiled. "Yes, but much better justice."

"Justice?"

Blue came over from his bed bringing his bone with him. He sat next to Anita and rested it on her thigh, looking up at her. "And who is this?" she asked.

"That's Blue," Dan answered. "He's friendly, trying to make you feel better by offering a bone."

"What a thoughtful fellow," she said, the whiskey helping her smile come easier now.

"You can pet him," I said.

Resting her glass on the bedside table, she reached out with her free hand and patted his head. He scooted closer, leaning against her, still holding onto his bone.

"What did you mean about justice?" I asked.

Anita sighed and lowered the ice from her face. "I guess I should start from the beginning. I'm an investigative reporter on assignment with a French magazine, *Something*."

Dan nodded. "I know it."

I'd never heard of it but I didn't like the sound of it. I liked my privacy and here I was face-to-face with a professional storyteller.

"What was the article?" I asked.

"I'm working on a book." She shook her head. "I'm sorry, this is coming out as a jumble."

"It's okay," I assured her. "Take your time."

Placing the ice pack on the bedside table she picked up her whiskey again and sipped from it. "You wouldn't have a smoke, would you?"

"Sure," Dan said. "Tobacco or other?"

She smiled and I saw her shoulders relax. "Both would be lovely."

"No problem," Dan said moving toward the desk. I shifted out of his way. Dan opened a drawer and pulled out a cigarette, leaned over and handed it to Anita. "Do you mind smoking it outside?" he asked.

"Of course not," she said rising.

"I'd keep that ice on a little longer," I said. "I don't know how many times you've had your ass kicked, but without that ice pack it's going to be a lot worse in the morning."

Anita turned back to the washcloth and picked it up. "Thanks again," she said, turning to me. Anita stared at me for a long moment and then asked, "Who are you?"

"I told you," I said, feeling uncomfortable. "My name is Sydney Rye."

"Yes, but you are not just some tourist. You're—" Her voice faltered. "I don't know. You're not police," she said, her intelligent eyes roving over my face, down to my hands which lightly held my almost empty glass. "But you're something," she said.

"That she is," Dan said, not raising his head from the joint he was rolling.

"I've had some training," I said. "But I'm retired."

"Retired from what?"

Anita looked like a reporter now; even with the ice pack pressed over her left eye, I could see the unquenchable curiosity coursing through her. The smell of hash floated through the room as Dan heated it up, crumbling it into the tobacco.

I smiled at Anita. "Let's go outside so you can smoke that cigarette." She opened her mouth to speak, but I hardened my eyes. "Don't push it," I said quietly.

She swallowed, blood draining from her face. "I'm sorry, of course, I owe you my life. Please forgive me."

"Sure. I don't think you need to tell anyone about me though, do you?"

Her mouth gaped. I opened the door and stepped out on the veranda.

She followed silently taking a seat on the bench by the door while I sat on the wooden swing. A cool breeze came off the water, and I was happy for my leather jacket.

Anita leaned forward and lit her cigarette off a candle burning on the coffee table. She leaned back and exhaled a plume of smoke with a throaty sigh. "I gave these up, you know?" she said, turning to me.

"Doesn't look like it to me," I said.

She laughed and finished off the last of her drink. "Tonight the chances of dying of lung cancer seem far off."

"Will they come after you?"

Her hand trembled slightly as she raised the cigarette back to her mouth. "I think so," she said. "He knows who I am now."

"Who?"

"Kalpesh Shah."

"Who?" Dan asked, standing in the doorway.

Anita swiveled her head to look back at him. "A very powerful, dangerous, and evil man."

"Evil?" Dan asked.

I stood up and brushed past him to grab the bottle of whiskey. I was going to need more of it if we were going to talk about good and evil. When I stepped back out Dan was swaying in the swing, smoke from the joint following his slow movements back and forth. He smiled at me and passed it over. I handed him the bottle. He leaned over and refilled Anita's glass.

I took a long drag off the joint, loving the taste of toasted tobacco and hash mixing with the whiskey fumes in my mouth. I leaned forward and passed her the joint. "Tell me about him."

Anita took the joint and inhaled, letting the smoke out in a plume that floated over the candle and dissipated into the night. "Kalpesh Shah is from one of the most powerful families in Gujarat," Anita began. "His parents died when he was sixteen leaving him a great fortune in the care of his uncle, Anand Shah." She took another drag off the joint. "A hard man, Anand beat Kalpesh and made his life a living hell." Anita leaned forward and passed the joint to Dan. "There is a scar on Kalpesh's face that runs from his temple to his jaw," she ran a finger down the side of her face. "The story is that Anand cut him with a broken beer bottle. I don't know if Anand molested Kalpesh, but I wouldn't be surprised considering his proclivities now. Anand raised the boy in his own image."

I felt a chill run down my spine. "Nurture," I mumbled.

"What?" Dan asked, leaning closer to me.

I shook my head then reached over and refilled my whiskey glass taking a long sip, feeling the warmth in my belly. The hash and the whiskey made my thoughts deeper, wider, they reached far and appeared rich, picturing the scarred boy and his terrifying uncle.

"When Anand died, Kalpesh was in his early twenties. He was the man's only heir and at least publicly grieved his uncle deeply. Never before had so many mourners been hired."

"Mourners for hire?" I asked. Dan passed me the joint, only a nubbins now. I took the last drag and then stubbed it out in a nearby ashtray.

"Yes, professional mourners. Simply, they cry for you."

I nodded, sitting back into the swing seeing black-clad, wailing women, writhing with imagined grief.

"His fortune is vast, and there is no reason for him to work. So he takes his pleasures as an occupation." Anita closed her eyes and leaned her head back against the wall.

"What pleasures are those?" I asked.

"Perversion, pain, children," she said, moving only her lips. "He buys them by the dozen, tires of them quickly, and releases them onto the streets with nothing more than the clothes on their back."

"Jesus," Dan said. He reached across the swing, squeezing my shoulder, pulling me closer.

"No one does anything," Anita continued. "He owns the police and even if he didn't, the rights of children are hardly a top priority," she said her voice bitter with truth. "They matter less even than those of women."

"Why is a French magazine interested in this Shah guy?" Dan asked.

Anita sat up placing the cloth wet from melted ice onto the coffee table. "Several years ago he 'hosted' the Paris Children's choir," she caught my eyes holding them. "They reported waking up without their clothing, groggy, and bruised. One of the chaperones disappeared, the other," she flicked her eyes to Dan, "spent three days in a drug-induced coma."

Dan shook his head and drank deeply from his glass. "How could he get away with it?" Dan asked.

"There is an extradition order for him, but like I told you, no one can touch him in Gujarat. He can do no wrong there."

"So what are you doing in Goa?" I asked.

She returned her intelligent eyes to me; they looked tired now, sad, but not defeated. A spark glowed in them that I admired. Kalpesh Shah was going to have to kill Anita if he wanted to stop her. "He has a house here. I heard that a shipment was coming, children from Nepal, new ones. He planned on staying at his estate a week, then returning for the kite festival but he was delayed in Gujarat. I was sneaking onto his property trying to get proof of the children. Take pictures, maybe talk to some of them. I got caught. You saw what happened next." She closed her eyes again and swayed slightly. "Thank God you were there."

"Then what?" I asked. "Once you talked to the children, got the pictures, what was next?"

"He has an open house every year for the Kite Festival. It's a family tradition that reaches back five hundred years. He can't refuse any guests. I planned on going there, getting pictures of his home, and speaking with him; that would be the final piece of the puzzle." She became animated now. "I already have a police source who's admitted on the record that they've ignored numerous accusations against him. And someone inside his household has been feeding me information. I'm so close." She sat back again, looking exhausted.

I fiddled with my glass of whiskey. "So what you need," I said, "is to get him on a plane to France."

"What?" she asked.

"If he landed in France he'd be arrested, right?" I asked, taking a sip of whiskey, feeling the fire in my belly.

"Yes," she said. "But...I'm a reporter. My plan is to expose him for what he is."

"In the French press?" I asked. "What will that accomplish exactly?"

Her eyebrows pulled together in conference over her elegant though swollen nose.

I leaned forward, feeling my heart beat in my chest. "I have a plane."

"You what?"

"I have a plane and I can get that murderous, child-abusing piece of shit on it."

Anita stared at me, speechless.

CHAPTER NINE
CHEMICALS

I laid under the mosquito net staring at the textured shadow it cast on Anita's sleeping form. She was breathing slowly, evenly, like someone who needed it. I knew I should rest, too, that my body deserved time to recover, but it felt like a live wire. Dan had offered Anita his side of the bed. Anita's exhaustion caught up with her soon after my declaration that I would grab Kalpesh Shah and drag his ass to France.

Why did I say I would go and get him? Because I could? It wasn't that simple. I wanted him stopped. The thought of those children being sold to him...I felt bile rising in my throat and sat up.

Anita rolled, stirred, but quickly settled back into her deep slumber. I slipped out from under the white gauze and tiptoed out of the room. Blue, of course, woke and followed me, his ears perked. I checked around the corner and saw Dan passed out in the hammock, his arms thrown wide, one foot hanging over the edge.

Taking a moment I watched his chest rise and fall. He was so sweet looking. His hair, always in need of a cut, flopped across his forehead. A thin sheet covered his body but I knew that it was sinewy, strong. And he was so damn smart, knew so much. So many nights I'd slept next to that man, laughed with him over coffee in the morning, played with him in the surf, yet I felt no ownership. Dan was not mine.

Quietly I headed through the trees to the pool. The lights were off and I slipped off my pajama pants, pulled my T-shirt over my head and, naked, dove in, making hardly a splash. Blue followed along the edge, watching me as I back-stroked from one end to the other. I switched to crawl and then finally to breast stroke.

Sober now, the cool water and exercise clearing my mind, I thought about Anita's story. She was brave, and no fool. I wanted to help, and not just because it was the right thing to do, but because I itched for something bigger than paperbacks and sunbathing. Mulberry and Dan were right about me. I couldn't live a quiet and safe life. I stopped in the deep end, catching the edge of the pool and floating against the wall.

Blue came over and touched his nose to my wet head. He licked at my eyeball, and I pulled away. He was recovering well, the stitches were dissolving, and all the puncture wounds closed. His hair was coming back, but he still looked patchy, not his usually gorgeous self.

The missing fur reminded me of why I tried to stay safe, not so much for me but for those I loved. Running after this Kalpesh Shah could get us all killed. My heart beat in my chest just thinking about Dan in danger. He never shied away from it, he'd been instrumental in taking out the last evil bitch I'd faced but if he was hurt or, I shuddered, killed, I'd never forgive myself. I had enough ghosts haunting me without Dan's sweet memory.

"Hey," I looked up and there he was, standing at the edge of the pool in just his boxers. He smiled at me. "Want some company?"

I nodded. "Sure."

He pulled off his pants and dove in. I watched his pale form elegantly glide through the dark water. He rose in front of me, his hair plastered to his head. He leaned back and dipped under again, this time his hair was off his face. He smiled at me, his gorgeous eyes bright in the moonlight.

Dan swam over and placed an arm on either side of me, holding onto the edge of the pool, letting the weight of his body press against me. "I like what you did back there," he said. *"I've got a plane,"* he said grinning. "You're just so fucking awesome."

I laughed and he kissed me, running one of his arms around my waist. My legs floated up and encircled his hips. Dan's kiss became more urgent. I let go of the wall and held onto his back, trusting him to keep us both afloat.

EK

After, we laid on one of the sun-beds, head to toe, wrapped in beach towels, staring up at the sky. He played with one of my feet, tickling the bottom. "Hey," I said, pulling it away.

A small smile played on his lips, his long lashes fluttered against his cheeks. "I'm proud of you," he said.

"What?"

He shrugged. "I like it when you're doing something."

"Yeah, I guess, me, too."

"You're going to let me help, right?"

I felt a tug on my heart. "Dan, I don't want you to get hurt."

He looked over at me, "I don't want you to get hurt either."

"Yeah, but I'm trained to not get hurt you're..."

He smiled. "A computer geek."

"Maybe that will come in handy," I said.

"So I can come with you?" he asked.

"Yeah, of course, you can come with me."

He grinned. "Good." I closed my eyes and leaned back, anxiety churning in my chest.

EK

We laid there in silence for a moment and then Dan wiggled my big toe. "What was your first boyfriend like?"

"What makes you ask?" I said, opening my eyes.

"I don't know," he looked up at me. "I guess I was just thinking about my first love." Color rose in his cheeks and he gazed to the ground.

"Oh really?" I said. "Now I want to hear about her."

"You first."

"No way," I laughed. "Come on, spill it," I pushed at his chest with my foot.

He smiled. "She was wonderful, older," his smile jumped into a quick grin, pride. "She was very pretty but tough, you know. She was a bad ass basically. She used to take me to the church behind our high school to smoke. She taught me how to roll those joints you enjoy so much."

"I should thank her," I said.

He laughed. "Yeah right." Dan reached out and played with my foot, rubbing at it absentmindedly. "I was two years younger than her and she took me under her wing. I followed her around like a puppy. We were just friends. But by the time she was a senior I'd had a growth spurt and was starting to come into my own. I felt powerful with the computer stuff rather than geeky." He laughed. "Actually, what happened is I got good looking. I noticed her notice. She'd always brushed up against me and been playful, teasing me; offering me something she knew I didn't dare to take. But then one day in the darkroom—that's how we met. We were both into photography."

"What did she look like?" I asked.

"She had black hair that she put colored streaks into. Wore a leather jacket and tight pants. She had a nose ring, a tongue piercing, and a belly button stud. She had tattoos. The chain connecting her wallet to her pants jingled when she walked. It was a sound I came to relish."

"So what happened in the dark room?"

His teeth flashed. "When we first met she would look over my shoulder at what I was doing and help me out. By the time we kissed she would ask me to come look at something and my nose reached the top of her head. She smelled exotic. She used Indian soaps from this crazy store in a strip mall. I love that smell to this day." He laughed. "It might be one of the reasons I like India so much."

"Okay, so you're in the darkroom smelling her hair. Then what happens?" I asked, teasing.

Dan laughed. "She turned around, but I didn't move. She laughed and said, 'Dan, a little space'. I just shook my head 'no' and stood there. I reached out and played with a strand of her hair, wrapping it around my finger. She looked up at me and we were really close. 'There's something

I need to tell you,' I said to her. She nodded and swallowed. I could feel energy vibrating between us. The way it had been for several months. She made me feel included and special and I worshipped her for it. I mean I really worshipped her."

"That's how you're avoiding the mistake with me?"

"It helps, and you're kind of a loser." He grabbed at my ankle and I kicked him away.

"Finish the story." He bit his lip and reached out again. This time I let him drag me toward him, wrapping my legs around his waist. He leaned over and sweeping aside my towel, raspberried my belly. I laughed and pushed at him.

"This is how I show my respect, Captain."

"Get off of me!" He tickled me until I wriggled out of his grasp. "I want to hear what happened. She turns around, you won't move, and then..."

"Okay, so I'm playing with her hair and," Dan licked his lips, "I told her I loved her. That I'd loved her since the day we'd met. My heart was beating out of my chest. And I could feel every nerve in my body. It was hot in there and the smell of chemicals thick. She raised onto her toes and touched her lips to mine. It was soft at first, then her tongue darted out and I thought I was going to pass out." Dan smiled at me, his eyes hooded and misty with memories.

"What was her name?"

"Morgan, but everybody called her Moe. I thought that was so cool."

"So how long were you together after the kissing in the dark room thing."

"Two years. Basically until I moved to California. And then she broke up with me. She was living in New York, went to NYU, and I had gone every weekend, religiously. My mom did not approve, but since my dad got me on the weekends and he thought banging a college girl was by far the best use of my time, he allowed it. Guy was happy to hear I could get a girl, considering my nerdy attributes. But when I decided to go to California for school, she called it off."

"Why'd you go that far away if you were in love?"

"I wanted to stay together."

"Obviously not if you moved away, if you left her."

"Maybe you're right," Dan said with a frown.

"Are you still friends?"

"Sure, yeah. She's a mom living in New Jersey. Crazy right? The coolest girl I ever knew ended up a mom in New Jersey."

"Coolest girl? Ahem. What about me?"

"You're no girl."

"Ha!"

"What about your first love? Your first heartbreak?"

"Morgan really broke your heart?"

"Yes, I was a total mope for a year. Now tell me about who cracked yours."

"I've never been in love."

"Really? You've never had your heart broken?"

I shook my head. "My heart is broken," I laughed ruefully, "now I'm just trying to avoid having it shattered."

"I guess," Dan said. He looked out at the water and we sat in silence for a while.

"Dan, you don't want to be with me," I said softly. "I don't know why you're sticking around. I'm no good." I felt a tear slip and rubbed at it quickly.

Dan reached out and pulled me to him. I let him wrap me in his arms, spoon me, kiss the back of my neck. "You are good, Sydney," he whispered. "You're the best."

"I'll only hurt you. I can't give you what you deserve," I said, feeling awful that I didn't have the strength to push him away, to save him from me.

"I only want you, as much as you want to give."

I shook my head, feeling his heart beat. "Dan, you don't understand."

He propped himself on his elbow, and I rolled onto my back so that I could see his face in the darkness. "Sydney," he smiled, "you really worry too much."

I laughed and he kissed me.

CHAPTER TEN
WHATEVER WE ARE

Dan and I were already at breakfast when Anita joined us. "You know when I woke up this morning, at the first crack of consciousness, I thought it was all a dream." Anita smiled. "But when I opened my eyes, Blue was staring across the bed at me and I remembered what happened. Though I'm blurry on some of the details at the end of the night." She leaned toward me. "Did you really offer to get Shah on a plane to France?"

I thought for a moment about not admitting it, but then Dan jumped in, "She did and she can."

"I'm a reporter, not a spy or a vigilante."

"A vigilante of sorts," I said. "You're exposing lapses in justice rather than correcting them, but we are both hoping for the same outcome."

"I'm hoping for the institutions that bind our civilization together to stand up and do what they are supposed to do. What you're talking about is different."

"Not that different. I'm just giving a helping hand. France's institutions will get a workout, I'm sure."

Anita sighed. "I'm sorry, at the moment my mind is really blown. Ever since those men caught me I've been stuck in some alternative universe. None of this seems real to me."

"Anything we can do?" Dan asked.

"I need to write some notes on what happened last night." Anita said to herself as much as to us. "I need to get that down and out of my head. I need to call my editor and let him know what happened. My bag is gone, those men stole it, so I've got no ID and I'll need that to get back to Ahmedabad. I don't have any money and..." she looked up at me, "you're saying that you can deliver Kalpesh Shah with a shiny bow on him into French territory. It all just sounds absurd and not at all what I was expecting. I thought I was going to die."

I put my spoon down onto the saucer of my coffee cup. "Yes," I said. "Doesn't it feel wonderful to be alive?"

She stared at me out of her bloodshot eyes. Her mouth opened and closed like a fish. "I suppose," she stuttered. "Yes," a smile slipped onto her puffed lips, "I suppose it's very nice."

Monica arrived with my pomegranate. "Would you like one?" I asked, gesturing towards the bowl of ruby seeds. "It's really perfect right now."

Anita nodded and Monica left to go get it. "Have some coffee," I said. Dan poured her a cup, and Anita stared at me.

"Put him on a plane, against his will?" Anita asked, picking up her mug.

"Yes, I imagine he wouldn't come peacefully." The thought thrilled me. I felt my fingers itching for the fight.

"Who are you, really?"

I took a bite of pomegranate and looked over at Dan. He was sipping his coffee and staring out at the river. "My name is Sydney Rye, and I can get that disgusting piece of shit on a plane to France."

Dan looked over at me and a smile crept onto his face.

Anita sat back and licked her swollen lips. She looked almost worse this morning. The bruises on her face had all puffed in the night. The bottle of whiskey we'd shared probably hadn't helped. "Can I write about it?" she asked.

I shook my head. "Absolutely not." She frowned. I sat back. "I can't imagine what your objection is here. The guy tried to have you raped and murdered, he's buying children to rape them. What's your issue?"

She glowered across the table at me. "I don't think it's as simple as you make it sound. How are you just going to 'grab him?'"

"At the Kite Festival."

"You're going to try to kidnap him at the Kite Festival in front of how many hundreds of people?"

"If he can keep a dozen kids hidden what makes you think we can't get him out of there?"

"He has security."

"Which I'm hoping you can tell me how to evade."

She bit her lip and then winced. "Shit," she muttered.

"Want some Advil?" Dan asked.

She shook her head. "I just don't understand."

"What?"

"Why would you do this?"

Dan laughed and we both turned to look at him. "Sorry," he said, shaking his hand.

"After you take him to France what will become of the children?" Anita asked.

"Sounds like a line from a Simpsons episode," Dan said.

"What do you propose we do with them?" I asked Anita.

"Don't you understand that as soon as you take away Shah you have an entire organization, an entire bureaucracy, the entire city, everyone who is in charge will want those children dead. They are the key, the evidence that will bring them all down."

"So I guess we get them out," Dan said. "I don't think we should not do this because we don't know what to do with a bunch of kids. There must be NGO's that will take them. I'll find somewhere."

"Right, then, that's settled," I said. God he was sweet and cute. Saving children. Jesus, what was wrong with me? Why didn't I just fall into this man's arms madly, insanely, stupidly in love?

Anita's tongue came out and touched the swelling on her top lip. "I've never done anything like this before," she said. "I guess it could work," she continued. "But, I want to write about it."

"Unacceptable," I said.

Anita opened her mouth to say something, but Monica arrived with her pomegranate. Then the Swedish couple showed up and sat at the table next to us.

"Finish your breakfast," I told Anita. "We can talk after."

Anita agreed, and once our dishes were cleared I asked her if she'd like to take a walk with me. When I picked up one of the walking sticks Monica had left by the gate, Blue pranced in anticipation. Lulu came and howled at us, hoping for an invitation. "Monica!" I called.

"Yes!" came her muffled reply from deep inside the house.

"Want me to take Lulu on our walk?"

"Thank you!"

Lulu sprinted halfway up the road and then turned back in a cloud of dust charging us at full speed, her ears pinned to her head, her mouth open in a toothy grin. Blue stayed by my side until I said it was okay and then he dashed to meet her. They circled each other and us, jumping up in the air and grabbing at one another's legs.

I started off down the road on my usual route. The lazy river wound through green fields of neatly planted crops. I pointed out a temple, pink and blue, framed by palm trees. A man wheeled slowly by us on his bicycle, which was piled high with plastic buckets and jugs. He rang a bell and called out his wares.

I waved to a neighbor who hung laundry in her yard. Lulu chased a chicken out of the road, and a rooster swooped down and chased Lulu back. "I'm afraid," Anita said, then paused for a couple more steps. "What I really want to do right now," she continued, "is just fly back to France. But at the same time I can't just abandon those children, this story. I have sources who have risked their lives to help. I can't ignore their sacrifice. I am afraid, but I want to keep going."

"Which direction?" I asked.

Anita looked up at me like it was a trick question. I laughed pointing to the split in the road. "Up the hill is steep, and Blue and I were once attacked by a pack of dogs there. But it's quicker and a better workout. The other way is longer, smoother, lots of houses, very safe."

Anita didn't answer. "This seriously is not a question of which direction you want your life to go in but rather how you'd like to spend the remainder of this walk. Uphill or flat?"

"Uphill," she said.

We climbed the slope, neither of us speaking, our breaths coming too rapidly for conversation. We passed where Blue bested the alpha. Lulu sniffed the ground but caught up quickly. There was no sign of the dogs.

When we'd reached the top of the hill I asked, "When it was happening, were you thinking about how you would write it?"

"No," Anita said.

"Were you thinking, I hope this gets exposed for the world to see; for the monsters these men are to be brought into the light of day; or were you just hoping that it would stop?"

"No," Anita shook her head. "I couldn't believe it was happening again."

I stopped. "Again?"

Anita looked up at me, her swollen eyes defiant. "Yes. Again."

"Who?"

"Kalpesh. When I was a kid."

"I'm sorry, Anita."

"He's the one who should be sorry." Her fists were clenched. "The monster." Tears sprung into her eyes and she turned away from me. The sun reached higher in the sky, shooting rays through the jungle in shafts of light akin to lasers. Blue pushed his snout into Anita's hand and she opened it, reaching to pet his head. She swiped quickly at her face and then grimaced in pain.

"I guess that's something that you never really get over," I said.

She shook her head and smiled. "Certainly spent enough on therapy though."

I walked over to a low mud wall that lined the road and sat looking into the trees. Anita joined me, sniffling. "How did it happen?"

Anita sighed. "Our families have known each other for generations. He is older than me by about a decade and it started when I was so young." She shook her head and rubbed her shoe into the dusty road.

"You know, I barely remember anything before it. That's how small I was."

"Do your parents know?"

She nodded. "That's how I ended up in England. They wanted to get me away from him."

"Jesus."

"Yes, you can imagine what that made me think." She looked back up into the trees. I followed her gaze and watched a black crow who cawed at another, high in the branches.

"A punishment?"

"Yes, I thought I was being sent away because it was my fault."

"You know that's not true now."

She turned to me. "Do I?" She frowned. "No, I don't know that."

"What did your parents say?"

"Say?" she laughed. "Nothing. They never said anything but they did get me therapy."

"Did it help?"

She shrugged. "I'm here. This is where it all got me. My ass kicked, almost raped, certainly abused, sitting in the jungle chatting with a..." she turned to me, "whatever you are."

"A friend?"

She laughed. "You don't strike me as the type to have friends."

I laughed. "You might be surprised what a good friend I can be."

"Certainly a good person to have on your side," she said, nudging me with her shoulder.

I nodded. "I can help you."

"Help me what?"

"Make sure it never happens again. At least not by him, not to anyone."

Anita's eyes filled with tears as she looked out into the jungle. Lulu barked at something that rustled in the brush. Blue glanced in her direction, but stayed close to Anita. "You know what I've been most afraid of, ever since I realized what he was, how he became like that?"

"What do you mean?"

She turned to me and grasped my hands. Her skin was clammy and the bruises on her face suddenly terrifying in the bright sunlight that caught her cheek as she leaned toward me. She swallowed. "I've always thought, what if I became like him? What if it's like an infection? He got it from his uncle and then he infected me. What if that's what I turn into?"

I shook my head. "Anita, you are here, in this jungle, talking to whatever I am, because you are nothing like him. You are fighting for these kids, not destroying them."

She bit her lip and then grimaced. "I don't know what I'm doing here."

She turned away from me and stood. I wondered about her parents. What kind of a person would let their child believe all the things that Anita thought? And they must have known what was happening. Why would any parent ever let their child near a monster like that? "Anita?" She looked back at me. "Do you have siblings?"

"Yes, a brother and a sister."

"Were they...?"

"I don't think so."

"You never asked?"

"We don't have that kind of relationship. We don't talk about anything real."

"But it's happening to other kids now?"

"Yes, not kids like me though." Anita played with the hem of her shirt. "They won't get therapy or anything else."

"What do you mean?"

She looked over at me. "He doesn't mess with kids who have anyone who cares. I guess the man learned to be more discreet. Now he buys the children like livestock and uses them much worse. And everyone..." she sneered, "everyone pretends like it's not happening."

"Why?"

She frowned. "I don't know."

I stared into the trees and chewed on my lip. "They don't see it," I said.

"Yes, they do."

"People don't see what they don't want to see." I stood up and wiped at my pants, dusting off the red-brown dirt that clung to everything. Lulu barked and circled me, excited to be back on the move. We started down the road again, Blue staying close to Anita's hip. We walked in silence listening to the birds chirp and the rustle of creatures in the brush.

"Is your family still in Ahmedabad?" I asked.

"My parents and brother live there, my sister is in America."

I looked down at her ring finger. Seeing my glance she held it up for me. A tan line marked where rings used to sit. "Not anymore," she said.

"Recently?"

She pursed her lips. "Yes, perhaps that's why I'm here. To escape him."

I stopped again and she turned back to me. "Not really," I said. "You're not here because of a husband who did you wrong."

"No, I did him wrong. I never should have married. Way too fucked up. It wasn't right to pretend I could love him forever, for real."

I felt a clench in my chest hearing my thoughts about Dan said aloud.

"So you came for closure?"

Anita laughed deeply. "God, yes. Wouldn't that be amazing. To close this. To end it. But that's, that's not possible." She looked up at the blue swath of sky above the road. "I'll never be free of him, of these feelings."

"Maybe not," I said knowing that she was right. I'd never be free of what happened to my brother. His murderer was dead but he still had a hold on me, still controlled my thoughts. Made me so angry, so danger-ous. Anita was right, it was an infection. "You know what?" I said. "If you can't get closure, I suggest revenge."

"Is that what you did?" There was that look in her eye again. That reporter's curiosity.

I cocked my head. "Can I trust you?" I asked.

She licked her lips. "You saved my life. I owe you forever."

I nodded. "Then yes, that's what I did." I started walking again.

"Did it work?" She asked, her eyes widening with hope.

I smiled. "Well, I'm in this jungle now, talking with whatever you are..."

She laughed. We came around a bend and the guest house was only a hundred yards away. A single story, Portuguese-style Goan home, its roof extended over the large veranda. At its peak, a paper star swung in the breeze, decoration left over from the Christmas holiday. A high wall, topped with broken glass that glinted in the sunlight, separated the house from the road.

"I've wished for his death a thousand times," Anita said. Her voice caught in her throat. "And I also missed him." She shook her head. "What a fucking psycho he turned me into."

"I know the feeling."

"You were?"

"No, the being a psycho thing, though. I know about that. About having crazy emotions that make you do dangerous things."

"Is that what you do now?"

"I don't know what I do now, but I know that I want to stop Kalpesh Shah." I turned to her, taking her shoulders in my hands. They were small, and I could feel her bones. "I don't like injustice, I don't like it when people let things happen. When they just sit on their asses and watch. If you let me, I'll help you bring him to justice."

She looked up at me. "Let's do it." And then she smiled in a way that made her eyes glow. The glint of revenge, I thought.

EK

I loaned Anita my cell phone to call her editor after I made her promise not to mention me. I left her out on the veranda and went into our cabana to offer her some privacy...or at least the illusion of it. Dan sat at his desk, leaning over his computer, a joint hanging from his lip. He looked up when I walked in. "Good talk?" he asked.

"I think so," I said.

"We going?"

I nodded. "Yeah."

He grinned. "Awesome. Come here." I crossed the room and took the joint that he offered me. "Check this out," he said, pointing to the screen. "It's him, Kalpesh." On the screen a middle aged man with a deep scar down the side of his face looked out at me. He was not smiling but appeared amused. Possibly at the ridiculousness of his own outfit. He was dressed up in robes and jewels that gave him the appearance of something ancient, out-of-date and well, ridiculous. "His family has been in development forever," Dan said, taking the joint back. I sat on his knee and he scrolled through some more pictures of Shah. "His house in Old City is a heritage site and he's buying up the whole area." Dan told me, handing back the joint. I pulled on it, watching as the images flashed on the screen.

"So he could be keeping the kids in any number of buildings?" I asked.

"That's right," Dan said, taking back the joint. He smiled at me.

"What?"

"I'm just saying. This is what it could be like. You and me working together." His arm encircled my waist and pulled me closer. "We can come up with a new name for it."

"Calm down," I said. "Let's see how this goes, okay?"

"Yes, Captain."

"Don't call me that!"

Dan shrugged.

Blue stood up and greeted Anita, who stood in the doorway, looking down at my phone.

"How did it go with your editor?" I asked.

"I didn't like lying to her, but I didn't mention you," Anita said, looking up at me. "I told her I managed to escape the attackers myself. She wanted me to come home immediately, but I insisted I stay through the Kite Festival."

Anita stepped into the room and sat on our bed. "I guess soon after that she'll learn the truth when we land in Paris with Shah."

"You still can't talk about me then. You can't ever talk about me," I said.

Anita turned to me. "Really? How am I supposed to explain Shah being there, the private jet, any of this?"

"I'm sure you'll come up with something," I said.

Anita stood up. "What? Do I suddenly work for you now?"

66

I rose off Dan's lap, ignoring his whispered plea for calm. "No," I said evenly, "but you owe me." I raised my eyebrows.

Anita's eyes narrowed. "Yes."

"So stop bitching."

Anita sat down again and I followed suit. "Fine," Anita said nodding. "You're right. I'll do whatever it takes."

"That a girl."

CHAPTER ELEVEN
ARRIVING IN AHMEDABAD

Our flight landed into the dawn of a hazy day. Pollution gave the morning mist a sheen. This was no soft, billowing moisture left by a cool night; it was the dregs, the smoke of an industrial dragon.

Anita directed our driver through streets crowded with confusion. Rickshaws, cows, dogs, cars, wooden carts pulled by stick-thin men all pushed forward. Horns chorused. We pulled up in front of a modern building that rose into the thick sky, appearing to have no top. Anita dismissed the driver and then hailed two rickshaws. "Just in case, I don't want Kalpesh finding out where we're really staying," she said, helping me into one of the three-wheeled, black and yellow vehicles. Blue hopped up next to me while Dan and Anita climbed into another one.

The driver gripped his handle bars and, twisting the throttle, directed the little bee-like vehicle buzzing into traffic. A string of limes and hot peppers swung from the rearview mirror, a silent, spicy prayer to keep us safe. The toot of our horn laid down the soundtrack as we maneuvered through the brightening morning.

The city that protected Shah revealed itself in glimpses. There was nothing in its visage that spoke to the evil that did not lurk here but rather shined. His name graced plaques on buildings halfway built, bamboo scaffolding shrouding the construction sites. Funny to think a man responsible for the destruction of so many lives could also be the builder of so many buildings.

The streets became narrower and the structures shorter and older. Anita and Dan's rickshaw stopped at the mouth of a slim lane across from a temple with steep steps that led to open doors. I watched as a woman climbed those stairs, holding her young son's hand. Anita paid her driver and then came over and paid mine. We waited for them to turn and leave before Anita led us away from the temple into a maze of narrow alleys lined with thick, crumbling walls. Food littered the streets, which were pot holed and stank of a thousand years of civilization. A cow with long ears and a grey and white coat stood in the middle of the lane, munching on some of the abandoned food. He flicked one of his giant ears at the flies that buzzed around him. Blue moved closer to me. "It's okay," I told him as we passed the cow, who didn't take any notice of us.

Glancing around and finding no one in sight except for the slowly chewing cow, Anita inserted a key into a big wooden door covered in chipped blue paint. With a satisfying click the lock opened and Anita pushed into a darkened room. "Hurry," she said. Dan, Blue and I followed her inside.

She closed the big door, leaving us in pitch darkness. She flipped a switch and a string of bulbs illuminated the room we stood in. It had a ten-foot high ceiling and walls painted a dark blue. There was no furniture and dust covered the tile floor. "I bought this place a couple of years ago with my brother," Anita said.

"Does he live in the city?" I asked.

Anita nodded. "But we hardly talk, we never really did."

"But you bought a place together?" Dan asked.

Anita smiled. "He thought it was a good idea but didn't have enough money. I helped out. But we bought it as a company, so my name's not on it."

"Good," I said.

"Yes, I've been staying here while researching this story." A look crossed her face. Perhaps she was realizing this was no longer just a story. Now it was a choose-your-own adventure. "This way," Anita said as she moved toward an open door to our right. We followed her into a kitchen. She plugged in a string of construction bulbs that looped across the room, illuminating an old wooden table with four chairs, built-in cabinets, and a new refrigerator that clicked over, almost as if in protest to being disturbed.

"Are your parents in town, too?" Dan asked.

"They do live here but they're out of the city visiting my sister in the States. That's actually their building we went to originally. Hopefully Kalpesh will think we are staying there." Anita pointed toward a darkened stairwell in the corner of the kitchen. "The bedrooms are upstairs," she said. "There is plenty of room."

Handing Dan a flashlight, she started up the darkened stairs, lighting our way with her own torch. The white beam of light caught the dust that floated in the still air. The steps were narrow and steep, curving up into the floor above.

We came out into a small bedroom. A single bed, neatly made, was pushed up against one of the walls. A wooden desk piled with paperwork faced a large window, its curtains drawn. Anita went and pulled back the drapes. Sun poured into the room revealing cracks as thin and elegant as a spider's web, that lined the floor and walls.

I watched as Anita dropped her bag onto the bed and then walked back over to her desk. I could picture her sitting there poring over notes, pacing back and forth trying to puzzle it all out; almost like a prisoner or a monk. Either way, someone paying penance in the hope of freedom. I recognized her obsession and worried again about her telling this story.

Looking up from her desk Anita pointed to another set of steps. "You guys are up there. And the bathroom is through there," she said, pointing to a door to our right. Dan climbed the steps first. We came out into a room with windows all the way around. Its walls were painted black, but the sun had bleached them into more of a slate grey.

A double bed with clean white sheets on it sat in the middle of the floor which was painted ochre, also bleached by the sun. Dan dropped onto the bed and immediately pulled out his laptop. I walked over to one of the windows and pushed aside the white curtains. Rooftops spread before me. We were in the center of the old city. A rim of taller buildings surrounded the enclave of three and four story homes. Most of the roofs seemed in disrepair, many were corrugated steel, but a few sported fresh new tiles.

Anita came up behind me and looked out the window. "Shah's place is that way," she said, gesturing with her chin. "The parapets provide some shade," she said, pointing to a low wall that separated two rooftops. "The ladies will sit on mattresses while the men fly the kites."

"Women never fly them?" I asked, imagining women in bright colors laying in the shade while men and boys flew kites.

"Some do. I did," Anita said.

I glanced at her and she was smiling, looking out over the rooftops. "Were you any good?" I asked.

She laughed and turned back into the room. "Yeah, I was pretty damn good."

"Sydney," Dan said, and we both turned to him. He was looking down at his computer screen. "I got an email back from a woman at one of the NGO's I contacted. She wants to meet."

"Okay," I said. "Where?"

"At her offices." He started typing. "I'll tell her we can come today, right?" Dan glanced up at me, and I nodded.

CHAPTER TWELVE
FEAR IN FAITH

The Better Indian Children's Fund offices were in a dusty building in a shabby neighborhood without sidewalks or traffic signals. At the entrance, broken tile was piled up next to bare cement steps in what looked like an abandoned plan to refurbish the facade.

After exhaustive research Dan had come to the conclusion that they were our best bet. Founded by Chloe Denison, an American who'd originally landed in India with the Peace Corps, the organization cared for street kids, educating them, and offering a safe haven. From what Dan could find they were clean, broke but clean.

Chloe Denison, a slight woman with white-blonde hair and eyelashes that were almost clear, looked over the rim of her large glasses at us. She was in her early thirties, fine lines radiated from her pale blue eyes and dark circles showed how little she slept. Her tongue, pink and wet, curled out of her mouth, running across her lips in a nervous gesture.

Dan and I sat across from Chloe, a large desk piled with paperwork between us. Blue was by my side, his neck long, craning to see over the stacks of files. Chloe picked up a pen and fiddled with it. We'd told her we knew of some kids that needed help and that we wanted to bring them to her. "What are you going to do about Kalpesh Shah?" she asked.

Dan and I looked at each other and then back at her. She shrugged. "You don't think I know what you're doing?" She put down the pen and looked at her hands. "You think you're the first to try?"

"I'm sorry," I said. "What do you think we are going to do?"

She looked up at me through those pale eyelashes, her long delicate fingers entwined on the desk. "I've been here a long time. You're after those kids he's got locked away."

"How do you know-" Dan started.

Chloe waved him off, leaning back in her chair, and pushing her glasses up her nose. "I deal with homeless and abused children, and you think I don't know about what's going on over there?"

"All right," I said, "and what are you doing about it?"

A flush rose on her cheeks. "What do you think you can do about it?"

"Apparently, you're the expert," I said. Blue shuffled closer to me, leaning his haunch against my shin.

"I need to know what you're going to do about Kalpesh Shah," Chloe said. "If you think I'm risking..." She shook her head. "Not going to happen."

Dan sat forward. "As I told you in my email we are interested in making a rather large donation to this institution-"

A knock on the door interrupted him. Blue stood. "Come in," Chloe called.

The door opened and a tall man with dark hair, olive skin, and a Spanish accent walked in, talking and looking down at a clipboard. "I'm not sure we'll have enough—" He looked up then; seeing Dan, Blue, and I, he smiled and blushed. "I'm sorry, I did not realize you had visitors."

"Father Agapito, this is Sydney, Dan, and," Chloe paused for a moment before remembering, "Blue." Agapito reached out his hand and I shook it. He had calluses like a man who worked hard. "Pleasure to meet you," he said. Then reached out to Dan who stood slightly to make the connection. "I'm so sorry to interrupt." Agapito looked at Blue and smiled. "What an incredible creature. May I?" he reached his hand out.

"Sure," I said. "Blue." I nodded at Agapito and Blue offered him the crown of his fuzzy head. Agapito pet it gently. "Wonderful," he said.

"We were just discussing a topic you might be interested in," Chloe said.

Agapito looked at her. "Yes?" he smiled. "How can I help?"

"They are looking to place some abused children."

He frowned. "I'm sorry to hear that," he said. "It is so horrible when the weakest among us are taken advantage of." Agapito looked down at Blue for a moment and then raised his head. "Would you like to see our school?" he asked.

Dan and I looked at each other, both sensing that the tense conversation with Chloe could use a break. "Sure," Dan said, standing.

"It's only a couple of blocks away," Agapito told us. "We are full, but I'm sure that we can find room for the children you seek to help. Never have we turned any away."

He held the door for us, and we all reentered the hall with its institutional gray carpets and bare, scuffed, white walls. Agapito ran a couple steps to pass us and open the tinted glass doors that led to the street. The day had gotten hotter, and by the time I reached the bottom of the steps I felt sweat on the back of my neck.

I pulled my hair into a pony tail and reached into my bag, taking out my sunglasses and putting them on. Blue's tongue slipped out of his mouth and he began to pant. Agapito led the way through congested streets, most without sidewalks, putting his hand out to stop the traffic for us to cross. "You're quite the shepherd," I said.

He laughed easily. "Yes, and you are good with the puns. That is the word, yes?" A little girl ran up to us, snot crusted on her face and dirt smudging her smooth, youthful skin.

"Father," she said. "Want pencil, Father." She smiled up at him, ignoring the rest of us.

The priest grinned and, reaching into his back pocket, pulled out an orange-colored pencil. "How about this?" he asked. The little girl's eyes widened at the sight of the prize.

"Yes, Father." She reached up for it and then added quickly, "Please, may I?"

Agapito nodded and handed over the pencil. The girl ran away but then stopped a couple of paces and turning back yelled, "Thank you, Father!" Then sprinted away.

Agapito smiled watching her go. "Pencils?" I asked.

"Oh yes," he said. "They love them. Notebooks, too. You should see what these children draw. Amazing."

We turned a corner and half the block was taken up by a large, European-style church surrounded by lush green gardens. It looked out of place in the dusty busyness of the street. A man wearing only a lungi and a pair of flip flops pulling a two-wheeled wooden cart filled to comedic proportions with metal pipes spotted Agapito and grinned, showing off a mouth only half-full of teeth. "Hello!" he yelled.

"Hello," Father Agapito yelled back with a big wave.

"How are you?" the toothless, bare-chested man yelled, the words sounding foreign in his mouth.

"Very good! And you?"

Horns honked at the two-wheeled cart's progress but Agapito's friend continued his slow pace. "Very good! I am very good!"

Agapito waved at him again and then turned and opened a low metal gate for me. "Please, come in," he said.

I stepped into the shade of a tall tree onto a stone path. It led through green grass shorn short to the church's large wooden front doors. Blue sniffed at the grass intently. It was as if we'd entered a different world. The madness of the Ahmedabad street continued just on the other side of the gate. In fact, a cow reached his head over and crunched on the sweet grass, but on this side there was a quiet and peace. The air was actually easier to breath.

I looked over at Father Agapito. He was wearing a button-down white linen shirt and a pair of jeans with dark leather sandals. A thin gold chain disappeared into his neckline. The man was good-looking and young, younger than me, I realized. He closed the gate and then something across the street caught his eye. I followed his gaze and through the cacophony of vehicles, dogs, cows, and people, I saw what he was watching. A man, clearly angry, was yelling at a woman who cowered in front of him.

The man grabbed the woman by the shoulders and shook her. Then his hand came up and whacked across the young woman's face. She would have fallen if he had not been holding her up. Agapito leapt over the small gate and raced across the street, dashing in front of scooters, sliding over the hood of a stopped car and pushed between the couple. "Oh shit," I said.

Blue watched intently by my side, and Dan stepped next to me. "That's not your average priest," he said.

"No, no it's not," I answered as we watched Agapito speak slowly to the man. The woman reached out and scrunched the back of Agapito's shirt between her fingers. The young priest reached an arm behind him and lightly touched her sleeve, reassuring her, while using his voice and personal power to calm down her abuser.

"I've never met anyone like him," Chloe said. "The first time I saw him pull something like that I thought for sure he was dead." She shook her head. "But I was wrong."

I watched in awe as Agapito laid his hand on the man's shoulder and then, turning his body to create a bridge between the two, put his other hand on the woman and they all bowed their heads to pray. I would have just cold-cocked the mother fucker. I wondered which method was more effective. "Has he hit her before?" I asked.

Chloe shrugged. "I don't know. I've never seen them before."

"I didn't realize yours was a religious organization," I said.

"We're not," Chloe answered. "But we work closely with the church. They have the space and the energy."

"How long has Agapito been here?" I asked.

"We've worked together for two years. He approached me actually. Wanted better teachers, better funding, better results. But he can be unrealistic."

"I could have guessed that," I said.

Agapito shook hands with the man then blessed the woman, laying his hands on her head and shoulders. Saying his goodbyes, he crossed the street to us. It was as if the traffic parted for him. "Moses style," I said.

"What?" Dan asked.

I laughed. "Nothing."

"I apologize," Agapito said as he opened the gate for himself. "Shall we go in?" He raised a hand toward the church entrance.

Chloe and Dan started down the path, Agapito, Blue, and I followed. It was cool and dark inside the church. A large stained glass window depicted a man with his hand up, thumb pressed to his pinky and ring finger, the other two pointed up in a *tisk tisk* gesture. The Saint was balding with raised, judgmental eyebrows, and an outfit covered in crosses. It reminded me of my stepfather, who was fond of wearing a tie patterned with crosses. He called himself a priest but he was nothing like Agapito, more like the guy in the glass, judgmental and covered in meaningless symbols.

Agapito followed my gaze. "I do not like that depiction of St. Nicholas. He looks as if he is admonishing us, doesn't he?"

I nodded. "That's just what I was thinking."

"I would get rid of it, but there are much better ways to use our limited funds. Come, I will show you." We walked down the aisle between pews of dark wood, all with prayer books and hymnals tucked into the backs.

I never attended church as a child except with friends. My mother did not find her religion until I was a teen and by then she would have had to use chloroform to get me into her fiancé's mega-church of rip-off-hood. I thought back to the last time I'd seen her when I was in the hospital and James had just been murdered. She told me James was going to Hell because he was gay and I hated her for it. I hated her so much I thought I might explode with grief and pain. Her abandonment of James for how nature made him brought bile to my throat in that church as I walked toward the altar. Blue tapped his nose to my hip reminding me he was there, and I pushed the memory away as we turned and headed for a side door.

Above the exit a plastic Jesus wearing a crown of thorns, the blood at his hands and feet looking almost sticky in the low light, stared down at me, forlorn on his cross. I paused for a moment and Agapito stopped with me. "Do you have a relationship with Jesus?" he asked.

"Yes," I said. "But it's not a good one." I passed through the door that Chloe held open for me. The sounds of children's voices filled the hall. Both of Blue's ears rotated forward. As we walked over worn linoleum and passed closed doors, the voices and squeals grew louder. "The children are out in the yard," Chloe said. "We built it last year." She smiled over at Agapito.

"It is so wonderful for them to have a safe place to play," Agapito said. Chloe pushed open a door at the end of the hall and sunlight blinded me for a second. We stepped out into a walled yard filled with playground equipment covered in children. They pushed each other on swings and flew down the slide, which glinted bright silver in the sun. Kids crisscrossed the yard in what looked like a game of tag. Several young women in kurtas and jeans watched over them. A young boy, maybe seven or eight, raced up to Agapito and grabbed his hand.

"Come play, Father?" the boy asked.

Agapito crouched down. "Not now Goyo, we have guests. Can you say hello to them?"

The boy looked over at Dan and me, squinting against the sun. Then he looked at Blue. "Hello," he said with a shy smile. Blue laid down, kicking one of his back legs out, and panted at the boy.

"Hi," I said.

"Nice to meet you, Goyo," Dan said, extending his hand. The boy looked at it and then grinned. Taking Dan's hand he shook it extravagantly, pumping his little arm up and down.

"Nice to meet you, sir," Goyo said as if it was something he'd heard in a movie. Then his gaze returned to Blue.

"You can pet him," I said.

Goyo dropped Dan's hand and inched closer to Agapito, that shy smile catching his lips again. The boy shook his head, wrapping tiny fingers around the priests wrist.

Agapito ruffled Goyo's hair then sent him off to play with his friends. Once the boy was out of earshot Agapito told us, "His entire family died in a fire. I found him on the street, hungry and terrified." The priest smiled at me. "I am so pleased that I had a place for him here where he can eat, play, learn, like all children should."

"Yes," I said. "This is very nice."

"Come, I will show you our art room," he said, excitement edging his voice higher. "Perhaps my favorite place."

Chloe held the door for us and we stepped back into the church. Agapito opened the first door on our left and flicked on a light switch, bringing the florescent tubes that lined the ceiling to life. Large windows covered two walls. To our left we could look out onto the playground. The front windows faced a garden and beyond it a quiet residential street.

In the room were four long tables with cans of pencils and markers spaced out on them. A corner was set up with easels around a still life of pomegranates and jack fruit. The smell of paints and paper took me back to my high school art room. A place I always felt safe. Outcasts and bad asses are always welcome where paint and brushes reside. I walked over to the easels and looked at the paintings. One was by far superior to the others. I felt that I could reach out and touch the spines of the jack fruit depicted there. "This isn't a child's," I said.

Agapito laughed. "No, I will admit that is mine. Do you paint?"

I shook my head.

"Perhaps you should." He laid a hand on my shoulder and looked at the painting with me. "It is good for the soul."

I felt a sudden sadness at his words and reached out, touching one of the brushes. Its soft bristles tickled my fingers. "I was never any good," I said.

"Improvement comes from practice."

"Yes," I said, thinking of the skills I did possess.

"Do the kids all live here, too?" Dan asked, looking out at the children in the playground.

"Yes, we have dorms," Agapito said, turning to Dan and dropping his hand from my shoulder. I missed the weight of it and was surprised by that.

"Can we see them?" I asked.

"Yes, of course," Agapito said.

"Where do you find your teachers?" I asked as we walked back down the hall, Blue heeling at my hip.

Chloe answered me. "We have a relationship with a nearby college. Most of our teachers are local women."

"Yes," Agapito said. "I will admit I harbor a dream that some of the children here now will return to teach." He blushed. "Wouldn't that be wonderful?"

"Yes," Dan said. "Awesome."

"Awesome, yes," Agapito nodded. "I like that word very much." Then he turned and started up a flight of steps. "We have two large dorm rooms, one for girls and one for boys," he said as we climbed.

Reaching the top, Agapito opened a door. He held it for me, and I stepped into a large room that ran the length of the building. It had wood floors and was lined with single beds, neatly made. In front of each one sat a chest. Blue trotted down the aisle, his nose to the ground, ears swiveling, checking, making sure there was nothing hiding. Most of the beds were decorated with stuffed animals. It smelled clean and fresh. Many of the windows were open, and the sound of the children floated up to us. A breeze blew through the space and fans on the ceiling helped move it along. "Nice," I said.

"I feel that for many the communal sleeping feels very safe. I grew up with my own room and often found it frightening and lonely," he said. I pictured the young Agapito in a large and shadowed bedroom, clutching his bedding, imagining monsters in the shadows. The children who slept in these beds had faced real boogeymen.

"The boys' side is the same," Chloe said. "We don't have any empty beds."

Agapito shrugged. "We always have room for a few more."

Chloe frowned. "But you can see how much we have at stake here." Agapito turned to her, his head cocked and a question on his brow. Chloe cleared her throat. "The children they are trying to bring here belong to Kalpesh Shah."

Agapito paled. "Thank God," he said, turning to me. "But how?"

Blue, finished with his survey, returned to my side. I swallowed and suddenly the room felt small under Agapito's penetrating gaze. Noticing my discomfort he said, "Come, let's go to my office where we can talk; I'm sure we will find a solution."

Chloe led the way back downstairs to a small office with dark wood furniture and big, comfortable, worn arm chairs. Agapito sat behind his desk, the white of the priest's linen shirt looked bright in the dark room. Sunlight filtered through a leaded-glass window, casting a flat light. Dan sat in one of the chairs and I sat in the other. Blue settled next to me. Looking around at the space I tried to think of where to begin. A part of me wanted to run from the church and leap over that little gate. There was so much in the dogma of this institution that filled me with loathing, but when I looked over at Agapito I saw an undeniably good man.

"Do you hate gay people?" I asked.

The priest looked surprised for a second and then smiled. "Of course not, I hate nobody."

"But do you think they are going to Hell? Do you think they deserve to burn for eternity?"

"This seems off topic," Chloe said.

I turned to her. She was leaning against a low filing cabinet, her hands curled around the edge. Chloe wet her lips and then bit down on her lower lip under my gaze. "It's not *off topic*," I said. "I'm trying to decide who to entrust with the lives of children, and if it turns out one of them is gay, which is statistically almost guaranteed, I don't want them to grow up thinking there is anything wrong with that. Their heads have been fucked with enough. They don't need some bullshit fake morality stuffed down their throats."

Chloe swallowed and looked down at her feet. "Of course not, but," she looked back up, her glasses reflecting the windows behind me, "you do realize that this is India. It's only just become legal."

I turned back to the priest. "Look, you seem like an exceptional man with compassion and empathy. You obviously have a way with people. What I want to know is do you accept them for how God made them, or are you a hypocrite?"

"I am gay," he said. Chloe took a sharp intake of breath and the priest continued. "Obviously, I am celibate but I am gay. And I don't think I'm going to burn in Hell." He smiled at me.

"Is that only because you're abstaining?"

He shook his head. "Jesus wants us to love each other, care for each other. I make no judgments, but only want to help people find peace in this life and the next."

"However, that is not the standard line for the Catholic church. How do I know you won't get shipped out of here and another priest, one not as enlightened as you, comes in and fucks it all up?"

"I suppose you will just have to have faith."

"Not good enough."

"I will alert you if I ever leave. And, of course, Chloe's organization, which I'm sure you know is secular, is responsible for the majority of the school's curriculum and policies."

I sat back into my chair and held his gaze. He sat calmly but his eyes made me a promise I trusted him not to break. "OK," I said.

"Good," he sat forward. "Tell me about the children."

Dan spoke first, "I'm not sure how much you know about Kalpesh Shah and his," Dan paused for a moment searching for the right words, "ways."

Agapito nodded. "I have tried to save those children since I heard of them but have always failed."

"Our methods probably differ from yours, Father," I said.

"Yes." He looked down at his hands. "Do you plan to kill him, then?" he said, raising his head, making eye contact. The man's brown eyes glowed in the soft light.

I shook my head. "No, but I do plan on taking him out of the country against his will. Do you have a problem with that?"

The priest shook his head and then smiled. "There is nothing in the scriptures that tells us not to move criminals from one jurisdiction to another. Will you take him to France?" I was surprised by the depth of the man's knowledge and it must have showed on my face. "Sydney, you will remember that it was a Catholic choir the man abused. Before my time, but it is not something we forget."

"So you will take the children and care for them?"

"Those that will come," Chloe said. "The older ones," she shook her head frowning, "you won't get near them." She pursed her lips. "Once they reach a certain age, they won't let us help them."

"But you'll take in anyone who wants to come?" I asked, leaning forward.

"I don't know how many we can fit," Chloe said. "And what if you fail? What if he comes after them? It will put all the children in danger."

Agapito waved his hand. "We will take them and we will protect them. This is a great opportunity for good."

"Except-" Chloe started, but the priest shook his head.

"The Lord has led Sydney and Dan to us so that we may aid them in this most noble of tasks. Fear will not deter us."

Chloe bit her lip and nodded but I could see she was scared.

"I'm glad we are on the same page," Dan said. He looked over at me. "We should discuss the size of the donation." Turning back to the priest he continued, "What will you need to care for these children?"

"How many do you think he has?" Chloe asked.

"About a dozen, we think," I said.

"I know more are arriving tonight," Agapito said. "And he will be releasing several."

"What? How do you know that?"

"I told you this situation has worried me greatly since I learned of it. So I've made it my business to know what was happening."

"You have a source inside his household?" I asked.

"Where my information comes from is not of consequence."

Chloe spoke up. "I can do some math with a couple of different scenarios and get back to you. When do you plan on bringing them?"

"The night of the Kite Festival," I said.

The priest nodded. "Yes, there will be many distractions."

"But that is only three days away," Chloe said. "That's not much time."

"We can get you some cash right away," Dan said. "So that you can buy beds, clothing, whatever you think you need. Then we can do a larger transfer once you've figured out the long-term costs."

Chloe chewed on her lip some more but nodded in agreement.

"What about the boys being 'released' tonight? What does that even mean?" I asked.

"He doesn't sell them," Chloe said. "After Shah is done with them he gives them their freedom."

"Freedom?" Agapito said softly. "Perhaps from his house, but not his influence. I've talked with many of the older boys. Tried to bring them here but am always rebuffed. I will go again tonight though, if I can find them."

"Let me try," I said.

He cocked his head. "How many languages do you speak?"

"Only English, but I have a friend who speaks a few more," I said, thinking of Anita. "She will translate for me."

"It can't hurt," Chloe said.

Agapito nodded. "Yes, it will be good for you to speak with them. Perhaps your influence will be greater," he said with a sad smile.

"We should get going," Dan said, looking at his watch. "I'll get in touch once we have more information and Chloe, send me your banking information, I'll arrange for the first transfer today."

Agapito stood and the rest of us followed. "We'll show you out," he said.

As we walked back through the nave to the front entrance Dan paused. "You know what? I should probably run to the bathroom before we go."

"I'll take you," Chloe offered.

Agapito, Blue, and I stood under the reproachful gaze of St. Nicholas and waited for their return. The priest tilted his head up and looked at the large stained glass portrait. "How much would it cost to replace him?" I asked.

He smiled and shook his head. "It would not be worth it, there is so much else to do."

"Doesn't he bother you?"

"No, it is good to be reminded of how our teachings can be twisted into judgment." Agapito reached into the neck of his shirt and pulled out the gold chain that hung there. On the end was a small coin. He held it out to me, and I stepped closer to see it in the church's dim light. There was an image of a man stamped into the gold. "St. Nicholas is my patron saint," he said.

"Like Santa Claus?" I asked.

Agapito smiled. "In fact, you are right, that he is the basis for the Santa Claus myth. A generous man, he was known for bestowing gifts without anyone's knowledge."

I looked up at him. "How can you be known for something no one knew you were doing?"

"It is harder than you think to hide one's goodness."

I stepped back and leaned against one of the pews. "So what makes him your saint?"

"I picked him."

"Is that how it works?" He bobbed his head side to side in the Indian gesture of yes, no, maybe. It was a culturally specific form of communication and impossible not to pick up. "So why him? Because of the presents?" I smiled.

"You might think," he said with a smile. "But no, he is the patron saint of children. One of the miracles he performed was resurrecting three children who'd been murdered and put into a barrel to brine by a butcher who planned to sell their meat as ham."

"Gruesome," I said.

"Yes."

"They were lucky that St. Nick showed up and brought them back to life."

"As the boys held by Shah are lucky that you have come here to free them."

"I'm not a saint," I said, "and there won't be any miracles performed."

"I do not think we see the world so differently."

"Except you believe in God and miracles, I don't."

"But we are both here. Might it not be our fate? God's plan?"

"I'm here because I brought myself here. Will," I said, "not fate." I smiled. "But if you want to think of me as God, I'm cool with that."

He laughed deeply. "Sydney," he said, closing the space between us and placing his hand on my shoulder, "you don't have to believe in God for Him to lead you. Nor do you have to believe in miracles to perform them."

The front door opened, a beam of sunlight shot down the aisle and filled the space between us. Then it faded as the woman who'd entered shut the door behind her. Chloe and Dan came back, and Agapito squeezed my shoulder before turning to the exit.

He held the door for us. "Thank you," he said, "I will see you again soon."

CHAPTER THIRTEEN
ROOFTOP ESCAPADES

When Anita opened the door for us, she peeked out and checked the alley. There was no one there. Anita hurried us into the kitchen, saying she had bad news. "My source at Shah's place just got in touch. They were supposed to release some kids tonight."

"We know," Dan said.

"How?"

"A very interesting priest told us," I said.

Anita frowned. "What?"

"He runs a school for homeless and abused children with the organization we went to today. I think that someone in Shah's house is a Catholic and goes to confession," I said.

Blue barked and I looked over to where he sat in front of the sink. He looked at the sink, then back at me. I picked up his bowl and crossed to the terra cotta pot filled with fresh water that sat on the sink's edge. Dan said, "He also told us the boys they are releasing are at an age where they would no longer accept help from an organization like theirs." Using a ladle I spooned fresh water into Blue's bowl. He pranced in front of me, his nails clicking on the floor with excitement.

Anita shook her head. "That doesn't matter because he isn't going to release them. They are going to be killed. Tonight."

"We can't let that happen," Dan said.

I paused as I lowered Blue's bowl to the ground. "What made them targets?" I asked. Blue whined at me.

Anita's eyes filled with tears. "I think it's my fault. My source says they're tightening security since I escaped. Kalpesh isn't worried but the head of his protection team thinks it's best, and so he's going along."

"Does your source have any influence over Kalpesh? Could he convince him otherwise?" I asked, placing the water dish on the ground. Blue lapped at it, and I realized how dry my own throat was.

"No," Anita said, her voice breaking. She turned away from me and slid into a chair at the table.

"Do you know what the plan is?" I asked, ignoring my thirst.

Anita looked up at me. "The people bringing in the new shipment, the kids I followed in Goa, they are going to take the older boys away and," she swallowed, "dispose of them." I sat down across from her. "Can we help them?" she asked, her hands reaching out toward me.

"Do we know where they are getting picked up, anything, how we can intercept them?"

"I know where they've been held in the past, but I'm not sure if it's the same place."

"Can your source confirm?"

"I asked but he was not sure."

"Where is it?"

Dan placed a glass of water in front of me and I drank from it quickly, feeling the lukewarm liquid wet my insides.

"I can show you," Anita said, drying her eyes. She led us up the stairs to our room. Walking over to one of the windows she pulled aside the curtain and, banging on the frame a couple of times, pushed the window up. Anita hooked a leg over and climbed out onto the slanted roof. I followed her, my head spinning ever so slightly when I glanced at the edge.

Blue whined as Dan climbed out. He jumped up on the ledge ready to follow when I told him to stay. Blue dropped back down to the ground with a grunt of dissatisfaction. "This way," Anita said, stepping nimbly across the roof. Reaching the edge she sat, swinging her legs over and slipped off. I felt a shudder before realizing that it was a short drop onto another roof below, this one flat.

Dan and I followed Anita who was already striding across the tar surface. The sun had set, leaving the sky a soft pink. Anita turned left, disappearing behind a wall. When we caught up to her, I saw that she was shuffling along a narrow ledge. Dan went first, his feet looking dangerously large on the thin ridge. Anita climbed onto an old wooden balcony that looked rotten and then ducked inside a building. We followed, feeling the creak of the balcony under our weight.

Inside was dark, the pink light left from the sun not strong enough to penetrate the dusty air. "This way," Anita said. She pulled open a set of doors and passed through them. Another wooden balcony, its railings soft to the touch. Anita climbed over and onto a ledge that carried us out to another open roof. We had to climb up a couple of feet to get on it. The tiles were still warm from the day's heat.

At the opposite edge Anita pointed down into an alley. "That door," she said. I saw a metal door set into one of the thick walls. All the other doors on the block were wooden, most with chipping paint like Anita's.

"You saw the kids in there?" Dan asked.

"Yes."

"What is it?" I asked.

Anita shrugged. "One of Kalpesh's buildings. He owns most of this neighborhood."

I sat down, calming the vertigo that was fucking with me as I stared down at the door. "All right," I said. "If this is what we've got, I'll stay here and watch. We need vehicles. Scooters would be best. And what kind of weapons can we get?" I felt for the lead pipe in the folds of my leather jacket. Touching it brought a sense of relief.

"I'm not sure," Anita said.

"What about scooters?"

"My parents have one that we could borrow. Their place is about a twenty minute cab ride."

Anita was chewing on her lip staring, down at the door. The sky slowly turned a deep purple. "You two go now," I said. "Get your parents' scooter and another if you can and get back here."

"What will you do if they come?" Anita asked, looking over at me.

"Play it by ear," I said.

"Keep your phone on you," Dan said. "I can trace you through it."

I smiled up at him. "Creepy."

Dan nodded. "That's the kind of man I am."

I laughed. "All right, move it you two."

They both nodded and started across the roof, when Dan stopped and looked back at me. "Be careful," he said.

"You, too."

After they left I laid down flat, feeling the warmth of the tiles run the length of my body. With the sun gone the air was turning cold, and I felt a shiver run through me as I thought about what was happening behind that metal door. A man on a scooter turned down the alley and drove past, stopping at the far end. He got off and a door opened, yellow, warm light pouring out. A woman in a pink sari stood there with a baby in her arms. The man embraced her and kissed the child who rewarded him with a grin and a giggle. They went inside, closing the door, leaving the street in darkness.

I checked my phone, twenty minutes had passed. The tiles were chilled and I sat up, pulling my collar close. The city's light pollution only let the brightest of stars shine through. The moon, fuller than when it smiled down at me the night I saved Anita, hung low in the sky. The rumble of a van engine brought my attention back to the street.

I watched it roll slowly down the narrow lane, splashing through dirty puddles and sending rats scurrying for the shadows as its headlights illuminated the broken pavement. My heart beat faster and when the van stopped right in front of the door, I had to squeeze my metal pipe to avoid standing up and pacing. Instead, I flattened myself to the roof, scooting as close to the edge as I dared.

The engine died and the headlights faded. The driver got out and, walking around the front of the van, went and knocked on the metal door. Seconds passed as the driver scanned the alleyway. When the door opened, fluorescent blue light spilled into the dark night. A giant of a man stood in the doorway. He and the driver exchanged a few words before a third man climbed out of the passenger seat and opened the van's sliding door.

He waved for the occupants to exit. The first was an impossibly small figure, stick-thin arms, black hair on a big head. Another one followed, this kid slightly larger but slower, earning him a smack that hurried him inside. A third child climbed out, still baby plump. My breath caught in my throat and anger flushed my cheeks. I ground my teeth, breathing in through my nose. I squeezed my eyes shut, unable to watch the boy, still unsteady in his steps, pass by the giant.

When I opened them again, a much taller boy was exiting the building, his head hung on a loose neck, his shoulders slumped in what seemed a perpetual state of protection. He climbed into the van and was quickly joined by two boys of similar size. All three looked young, but not as small as the three that had entered.

I couldn't let this happen, I thought. Belly crawling away from the edge I rose into a squat and ran across the rooftop, my vertigo forgotten as adrenaline coursed through my system, letting me pick my way between the tiles without making a sound. Reaching the end of the block I looked back at the van; its headlights glowed back to life and its engine growled.

No time to waste, I took a chance on a drainage pipe, using it to climb down the side of the building. It creaked in protest and loosened under my grip, plaster dust preceding me down to the ground. Safely on earth I pressed myself against the wall and waited to see the van pull out of the alley and turn left. I had about thirty seconds to follow before they'd disappear. Rushing back down the street I jumped onto the scooter left by the young father and using my pen knife cracked open the wheel base with skill my high school sweetheart would have been proud of. With steady hands I pulled the wires, stripped the black power cord to the metal and touched it to the white. The scooter rumbled to life. Wrapping the third wire around the other two I hit the accelerator and raced out onto the street.

It wasn't hard to spot the van even though it was so far ahead. It was large in a sea of smaller vehicles. I managed to catch up quickly but kept my distance, letting the city hide me the way it'd hidden the devil behind that metal door for far too long. My surroundings were just a blur, my vision narrowed on that dark van as it maneuvered slowly through the city.

We passed streets populated by families living under strung up pieces of cloth, their entire lives on display. The women wore saris of vibrant oranges and pinks with babies on their backs as they tended to food cooked over open fires. Naked, dirty children stood, pigeon-toed, staring out at the passing traffic. Soon the buildings were taller, the roads wider. The van pulled off the main road onto a residential, dead end street, shabbier than the rest of the neighborhood but still better than living on the street.

The building's cement facades were blackened from the pollution. I'd have thought they'd been through a fire if I hadn't noticed the soot stains that covered the city. The street was quiet, TVs flickered in windows and the smell of cooking food floated on the breeze. I waited at the top of the street, cutting my headlight. The van stopped in front of the only house with all its shades closed.

CHAPTER FOURTEEN
THE VIRTUES IN JUSTICE

I couldn't let them knock on that door. Right now I already had two, I was assuming armed, men to deal with. The driver got out and I hit my accelerator, racing down the street at him. He started around the side of the van but when I was about ten feet away he turned back toward me, the sound of my engine catching his attention.

I took a deep breath and right as I pulled up even with him I pushed off the scooter's floor, my arms out and launched myself at him. He fell hard and we skittered a couple of beats along the pavement. As we bounced I reached inside his open jacket and, finding what I thought would be there, pulled the man's gun from his holster and pointed it into his face as we came to a stop. But the guy was out cold.

I dropped and rolled to the front of the van, staying low. The guy in the passenger seat had a couple of options. Get out and have his feet shot or call for backup. Which meant I needed to go in there and get him. I steadied my breathing, thinking hard. The driver stirred and sat up, a look of incomprehension on his face. I aimed his gun at him from where I sat crouched in front of the van, the headlights backlighting me and making him squint.

Blood seeped from the man's hair, trickling past sunken brown eyes set in deep dark circles. He noticed me and stared blankly. "Hands up," I said. He did as he was told, revealing forearms pulverized by road rash.

The door of the building opened, and I heard a woman gasp and cry out softly. Looking under the van, I saw her bare feet step into the street. Her toes were painted pink and there were bruises circling her ankles. The ligature marks made me mad. A man's dark dress shoes and burgundy cuffed pants followed closely behind the woman. I heard the van's window roll down and the passenger said something in Gujarati I couldn't understand. The man behind the bruised woman answered him and then laughed.

The driver yelled something then. I assumed something along the lines of "she has my gun and is pointing it at me." The man at the door yelled something back and then laughed again. I had a feeling he wasn't taking me seriously. Another example of sexism getting someone killed, I thought to myself, then rolled under the van until I was even with the laughing man, laying on my back. The driver yelled but I pushed off, propelling myself out from under the van between the woman's legs, then the man's. Then I shot his fucking balls off.

His scream came two beats after the loud crack of the gun pierced the night. The woman screeched and looked down at me with wide, black eyes. The man was looking down at his crotch. He dropped the gun he'd been holding and grabbed for his manhood then crumpled to the ground, his face white with anguish and shock. I somersaulted backwards out of his way and into the doorway, raising to my full height with the woman still between me and the passenger. Her back was splattered with blood as was my face and chest. I grabbed her by the neck and shoved her to the ground, shooting through the open window at the passenger before he got off a single round. He fell into the driver's side, his gun still in his hand.

The woman was sobbing on the street, her long black hair covering her downturned face. I looked into the house and saw steps leading up. At the top several young women, none of them wearing more than a small robe, looked back at me with huge, terrified eyes. There must be more men in there, I thought. Ducking back into the street I checked on the kids in the back of the van. One of them was crying and clung to another. The third looked out at me defiantly. There wasn't anything I could do to this boy that hadn't been done, his eyes told me.

I opened the passenger door and pulled the dead man out, flopping him onto the pavement. The woman on the ground screamed anew and scuttled away from him on her hands and knees. Picking up his gun I shoved it into the back of my pants. I looked down at the woman and wondered what to do. She crawled away from me, speaking in a language I didn't understand. I started toward her and she put her hands up to block her face. "I'm not going to hurt you," I said. She didn't put her arms down.

The single headlight of a scooter turned into the street and I crouched behind the van using it as a shield. The scooter stopped and I heard Dan, "Sydney?"

"Are you okay?" Anita called.

"Stay behind the van," I yelled to them seeing a man, his shirt unbuttoned exposing a broad chest covered in tight black curls, push through the crowd of women at the top of the stairs. He was holding a big ass gun. I fired off a round hitting him in the knee; he fell, reaching out with his free hand to clutch the banister at the same time raising his gun at me. I leapt out of his line of fire. The van shook with the impact of the bullets. The blue paint dimpled, leaving silver holes on the passenger door.

Pressing against the side of the building next to the entrance I waited for him to finish. When the bullets stopped, the only sound was the inconsolable sobbing of the woman with the bruised ankles at my feet. She'd pulled herself into the fetal position. I strained to hear what the guy inside was doing.

Over her cries I heard shuffling steps as he made his way down to the doorway. Would he really just walk out and let me shoot him? No such luck, I realized, as his gun, an automatic, boxy, fast killing machine curled out the door toward me. Using my free hand I grabbed it and pushed his arm toward the sky stepping forward in one motion. This pulled him toward me and our bodies pressed close. He pulled the trigger, rattling both of our arms as bullets exploded into the sky. Screaming seemed to fill the air. I pushed my gun against his bare chest and pressed the trigger. The impact jerked us apart, but I managed to hold onto his gun arm as, even in death, he continued to depress the trigger. The man's weight pulled us to the ground, and I struggled to keep the machine gun clenched in the corpse's hand under control until all thirty rounds were gone.

When the last kick came I waited a beat and then released him and stumbled away. Now there were three dead men in front of me. Blood covered my chest, arms, neck, and face. Unzipping my leather jacket, I used my T-shirt to wipe at my eyes. Anita came around the side of the van and looked at me then down at the bodies. Her jaw opened and closed but nothing came out.

"Tell her I'm not going to hurt her," I said, using my gun to point at the terrified woman still in the fetal position. Anita didn't move. I walked around to the driver's side, noticing that the former driver was still sitting there with his hands up. Smart man. Dan, who'd been on the far side of the van, touched my elbow.

"You okay?"

"Yeah, it's not my blood," I answered. "We're taking them all with us. You're driving." I opened the driver's door. "Get the engine started. I'm going to have Anita help get them in the van."

"What are we going to do with them?" Dan asked.

I looked over at the door where one of the women, small enough to be a child, was stepping through the blood to get a better look at what was going on. "Free them," I said.

Dan didn't ask any more questions. He just climbed into the van and started up the engine. I went back around to where Anita was speaking softly to the woman on the ground. "Tell them they can come with us and they'll be safe," I said, pointing at the women with my gun. They all threw their arms up. "Shit," I said, lowering it quickly.

"It might help them trust you if you'd stop swinging that thing around," Anita said.

"If I didn't know how to 'swing' this thing around I wouldn't be able to help them, would I?" I said, anger edging my voice.

Anita stood up and brushed past me. Her face paled when she stepped over the machine gun-wielding man's body. I followed her in and listened as she quickly explained—in Gujarati and then in Hindi--that they could come with us. Several ran down the stairs and scurried over the bodies of their captors to the van but four waited at the top of the stairs, unsure of what to do. One of them came down and spoke with Anita. The others kept looking upstairs.

"Ask her how many more there are," I said.

Anita held a hand up to quiet me as the girl spoke quickly, her eyes filling with tears. I went and patted down the dead men looking for extra bullets and found a magazine on the passenger. I handed my almost-empty gun to Dan through the van window. "Don't let him get away," I said, tilting my head toward the driver still sitting in the beam of the headlights. Dan nodded, his jaw clenched. I pulled out the gun I'd stashed in my jeans, slipping the extra magazine into my back pocket. I felt for my lead pipe again and gave it a reassuring squeeze.

"Sydney?" Anita said. I nodded. "This is Esha. She says her sister is upstairs. There is a room where they," Anita swallowed, her face growing even paler, "prepare them."

"How many?"

She turned to the girl, who told her there were two men with her sister, one was the big dead man at our feet and the other was still up there. "Show me," I said.

Anita translated and the girl pointed up the stairs. I gestured with my chin for her to go ahead of me, then started after her. Anita stood at the bottom of the steps. "You're coming," I said.

She shook her head, fear chattering her teeth. "I can't."

"I need you to translate. Stay behind me." She didn't move. "Grow a set of balls, Anita." Her eyes flashed. "That's it. Get angry. You should be. This is beyond fucked up. Now here is your chance to do something about it." I turned back to the young creature in the tattered white robe whose sister was upstairs and nodded at her. She started up the steps again and I heard Anita following.

The three girls at the top of the steps let us pass. The whole house reeked of food and sex. We passed small, dingy rooms with bare mattresses on the floor. At the end of the hall one of the doors was closed. I noticed there was a deadbolt on the outside though it was not locked. I stopped. "Is there a john in there?" I asked. Anita translated. The girl shrugged and said something in Hindi.

"She doesn't know. She was in her room when everything started. That girl did not come out. It could just be that she is hiding."

"Call to her," I said. "Tell her she can come out. It's safe."

Esha yelled through the door. Shuffling came from the other side and then the door creaked open. A giant pair of deep brown eyes looked out at us from under elegant brows. Esha whispered to her and the girl shook her head. "She is not alone," Anita told me.

"Get behind me," I said. Anita took Esha's arm and moved her back down the hall. I made eye contact with the girl on the other side of the door and tried to make her understand that I was her friend. She nodded at me and stepped back. I kicked the door open, gun cocked, looking for my target.

A diminutive man with thin gray hair sat on the bed in boxers and a white T-shirt, his hands above his head. The girl whose room it was spoke quickly. Anita came in and translated that the girl was saying he was a nice man and did not deserve to die. "He is always very nice to her," Anita said.

I nodded my head. "Fine, tell her to get what she wants and get in the van."

Anita translated and the girl grabbed a few scraps of clothing out of a pile by the door and hurried down the hall. I closed the door and pushed the deadbolt into place, locking the gentle john inside.

Esha encouraged me to keep going upstairs. I followed her past another floor of rooms, all the doors open, the former occupants safe in the van, I hoped. The fourth floor was an attic-like space with curved walls and low ceilings. The last door at the end of the hall was closed and Esha pointed to it. "Yell to him that if he lets her go, we won't harm him," I said.

Anita called down the hall with my peace offering. A man's voice answered, it sounded scared to me. "He wants to know who we are."

"Why?" I asked. "Never mind. Tell him that his friends are dead and I'm going to count to ten. If the girl isn't out by then I will come and get her."

Anita relayed my message. When we didn't get a response I started counting down. "ten, nine, eight..." I flashed back on my brother counting, playing hide and seek when we were kids. Shaking the memory from my mind I continued. "Seven, six..." The door creaked open. We crouched lower into the staircase out of range of anyone standing in the hall.

A shell of a woman stepped into the hall. Bloody, raw wounds circled her ankles and wrists. Long black hair hung in filthy strands around her naked shoulders. Her body, completely bare, was a study in bruising: hand prints on her hips; blossoms of discoloration across her abdomen; her breasts showed a pattern of cigarette burns. When she shuffled close enough for me to see her face, I winced at the swelling and redness that surrounded her eyes and mouth.

The door closed again and the girl stumbled into her sister's arms. Esha caught her and without a word started dragging her down the stairs, Anita helping with the girl's weight. I stood there for a moment staring at the closed door. Then, hearing the whine of sirens in the distance, ran down the steps. When I got outside Anita was helping the girls into the van. Dan, white knuckles on the wheel, said, "Come on, we've got to go."

"I'll take the scooter," I said.

"Where are we going?" Anita asked.

"Better Indian Children's Fund."

"Will they be open?"

"Yes," I said, confident for no other reason than it was how it needed to be.

Anita slammed the van door closed. "I'll take my parents' scooter."

"Okay, go," I said to Dan. He nodded and then backed the van out of the dead end and turned into traffic.

"Let's go," Anita said, climbing back onto her scooter.

"I'll follow," I said. Her eyes narrowed as I walked over to the driver, still sitting on the ground and hauled him to his feet. He cried out in pain.

"What are you doing?" she asked.

"If you think I'm going to let that motherfucker up there live, then you don't know me yet."

I pushed the driver ahead of me using him as a shield as I went back into the brothel. "Wait!" Anita called.

"Get out of here," I yelled over my shoulder as I muscled the road-burned man up the steps. The sirens got louder as we slowly climbed back up to the top floor. The driver started crying about halfway up. "I'm not going to kill you," I said. This did not console him.

When we got to the top floor, it was as I'd left it. The door closed. Pushing the driver in front of me I got right up to the door and then knocked. The wooden door exploded with gunfire, shattering the boards and peppering the man I held in front of me. He leapt and jerked with the impact. I held him up by the tatters of his jacket and hunched behind him listening to the sickening splat of bullets thunking into him.

As soon as they stopped I threw him to the side and kicked the door hard enough to take what was left of it off its hinges. A man of medium build stood in front of me his attention drawn away from reloading his weapon. I shot him between the eyes, giving him a morbid bindi. The sirens were blaring close now. I heard yelling from downstairs and the sound of feet pounding up the steps. Crossing the room I tucked my gun back into my pants and threw open one of the windows climbing out onto the slanted roof.

It angled down to the house next to it and I skittered off it, leaping onto the building. I ran, headed toward the main road. At the end of the block I looked back and saw two cop cars and several men standing around them in front of the brothel. Looking at the window I had jumped out of, I saw a man's face appear. I flattened myself to the roof and belly-crawled along the edge, looking for a way down. Nothing but flat wall greeted me.

I spotted a skylight in the center of the roof and scooted over to it. Looking through its grimy glass I saw an empty kitchen, the dining table right under me. I heard footsteps and yells as the cops climbed out the window after me. With no other choice I stood up and fired three rounds into the glass, shattering it. A deep breath and I jumped. Landing with bent knees, I stumbled forward catching myself with my hands. I felt a prick as one of the shards of glass bit into my skin. No one came running so I assumed the apartment was empty.

Moving quickly I found the exit and ran down the stairs. An apartment door opened as I passed and an older woman looked out at me. She started to yell, but then noticed the blood splatter, the gun, and the speed at which I was traveling and closed her mouth. Stopping in front of the door to the street I took a deep breath and looked out the peep hole. Nothing. "You only live once," I said to myself and then opened the door slowly and glanced down the block.

"Hey." I turned my head and Anita was on the corner. "Come on," she said. I grinned at her and ran the few steps to hop onto the back of her scooter. The bike jumped forward and we blended into the traffic.

CHAPTER FIFTEEN
ALL MEN ARE FRIGHTENED

There was no light on in Chloe's window when we pulled up in front of the Better Indian Children's Fund offices. Climbing off the back of the scooter I waited for Anita while she pulled the bike onto its kickstand. Dan wasn't there yet but that didn't worry me. Traffic was a lot easier on a scooter than in a big van.

We knocked on the tinted glass doors. When no one answered I tapped with the butt of my gun, making a louder noise, but still nothing. "We should go to the church," I said.

Anita agreed, so we got back on the scooter and drove the few blocks to the church. The gardens were dark but there was light inside the building. It shone through the gabled windows casting triangles of light onto the grass. The street was quiet at this hour when most people were home eating dinner or watching TV. Anita parked the bike right next to the gate.

I zipped up my jacket, covering the blood splattered on my shirt. "Here," Anita said, pulling the seat of the scooter up and reaching in for a rag. She spit on it and then rubbed at my face. The towel smelled of gasoline. "There," she said, standing back. "You'd hardly notice now." She reached forward and swiped at my jacket, nodding to herself.

"Thanks," I said. Her face paled as she looked down at the blood-stained rag. I put my hand on her shoulder. "Keep it together. We've got more work to do tonight." She looked up at me, making eye contact. The swelling on her face was gone, but there was still visible bruising around her eyes and the cut on her lip held onto its scab.

"I know," she said. "I'm okay. I just didn't think..." She looked back down at the towel. "I didn't think so many people would die."

I bit my lip. "Sorry," I said.

She looked back up at me. "Don't apologize. I think you did the right thing. I just never would have..." Her voice caught and I saw tears well in her eyes. "I just couldn't do it."

"Let's hope you never have to."

She sniffled and wiped at her eyes. "I just hope that I'd have the strength."

I squeezed her shoulder. "You could. We all have a switch that gets turned on when we need it. If the time came, yours would click." She nodded, but didn't look like she believed me. "Trust me," I said.

A truck rumbled by and Anita turned to watch it. "Let's go," she said.

I opened the gate and we passed through. Anita pulled the big wooden doors open and we saw that a service was happening inside. Agapito stood in the sanctuary above the pews, only a quarter full at best. He was speaking in Gujarati and wearing the long black dress of a priest with the white spot on his throat.

Heads turned at the sound of our entrance and I stood behind Anita, trying to disappear. Most of the faces turned back to their charismatic Father, but I spotted Chloe in one of the front pews staring at me. I waved her over and she rose, hurrying down the aisle toward us. She wore a blue dress with cap sleeves. Tall and slim, Chloe would have been pretty if she didn't look as if she carried a large weight across her shoulders that dragged her toward the ground. I opened the door and stepped back out into the night. Chloe followed into the darkness.

"What are you doing here?" she asked.

"There is a long explanation for that," I said. "We should probably go back to your offices."

"What?"

"We don't have much time. We need your help."

"Are you in danger?"

"No, but Dan is on his way right now with a van full of people who are."

"But, we are not ready," she said.

"Chloe," I said, grabbing her elbow and pulling her close to me. "I don't have time for your shit right now. There are lives at stake. Now I will march back into that church and pull Agapito out from behind that podium and get him to help me, or you can keep this shit a little more subtle."

She nodded, her eyes scanning my face. "Is that blood?" she asked.

"Yes, let's go."

She followed me toward the scooter, "Anita, you ride, we'll walk," I said.

Chloe came easily, even hurrying along the broken pavement to her offices. She fumbled with her keys once the building was in sight. Her fingers shook and she dropped them. I swooped down and picked them up. "I'll do it," I said.

She didn't protest and we climbed the stairs to her tinted doors. Anita waited at the top of the steps. I unlocked the doors then looked up and down the street before stepping inside. Dan still wasn't there. A worry started to turn in the pit of my stomach.

Chloe hit the light switches and fluorescent tubes in the ceiling flickered to life, casting a blue light down on us. "My God," she said, seeing me in the light for the first time. "Whose blood is that?" I sighed. "What are you doing here?" she asked, fear edging her voice higher.

"I'm not going to hurt you," I said, but she backed away from me. "Look," I said, "we just rescued the boys Kalpesh 'released,'" I held my fingers up like bunny ears, "and some prostitutes at a brothel." It was hot in the hallway and I unzipped my jacket.

Chloe's mouth dropped open. "Why are you covered in blood?" she squeaked out.

Anita spoke up. "She did what she had to do."

Chloe looked over at Anita. "What?!"

I sighed again, feeling the weight of this explanation. "I had to kill a bunch of men. They were going to kill those boys and I couldn't let that happen," I said. "Can I use your restroom?" I asked, feeling the itch of blood drying on my skin, tightening on it, feeling like a mask. Without waiting for an answer I turned to Anita. "Call Dan, will you? Get his ETA."

"Sure," Anita pulled out her phone and I turned back to Chloe.

"The bathroom?"

She pointed down the hallway, her eyes wide and mouth forming into a little 'o' of surprise. The door was marked with a pictogram of a toilet. It was a single stall with white tile walls and floor, a streaked mirror, and a western toilet. Locking the door I went to the sink, turning on the warm water and then looked up at myself in the mirror.

Anita had done a pretty good job on my face. There was just one line of blood that ran down my left side, close to the hairline, and a sprinkling across my cheek. My T-shirt looked like a Rorschach test; I saw two bunnies fighting viciously. Taking off my jacket I hung it on a hook on the door and turned back to the full sink. I splashed the warm water on my face, rubbing it into my hair. Pulling reams of paper towels out of the dispenser, I rubbed at my cheeks and hair until my skin was pink and clean.

I shrugged out of my T-shirt feeling the strain in my shoulders from all the kicking of fired guns. Putting it in the sink to soak, I wet more paper towels and went at my leather jacket, cleaning off the blood and bits of flesh stuck to it. My stomach churned for a moment, but I pushed it all down into my gut and kept cleaning. This was no time to get squeamish.

Pulling my T-shirt out of the pink water, I saw it was hopeless and dropped it into the trash. Once I'd done all I could for myself and my clothing, I reached into the lining of my leather jacket, past the lead pipe, to where I'd stashed cash. I pulled out five thousand dollars in hundreds, everything I had in there. I put five hundred dollars back in the lining and jammed the rest in the back pocket of my jeans. If I couldn't reach Chloe through her conscience, I hoped to entice her with cash.

I put my jacket back on over my bra and zipped it up. I found Anita and Chloe in Chloe's office, drinking Old Monk rum. They both looked pale and in shock. "God, I'll take a drink," I said. Chloe gestured toward the bottle, pushing a plastic cup toward me.

"Dan had to pull over to check his phone for directions and one of the boys ran for it," Anita told me.

I clenched my jaw in frustration. At least he was alive, I thought, as I poured myself two fingers of rum. "Is everyone else okay?" I asked.

Anita nodded and drank deeply from her glass. I turned to Chloe. "Did Anita explain who's coming?"

Chloe nodded and removed her glasses, squeezing at her eyes with her free hand. I pulled the money out of my pocket and when she opened her eyes I held it out to her. "This is to help with them. I'll get you more."

"We don't usually work with adults," she said as much to herself as me.

"I know, but you must know someone you can trust who can help these girls. Several of them are going to need medical attention. Do you have any doctors you can trust?"

Chloe nodded. "Yes, I think so." She picked up her phone and then put it down again. "You realize that anyone I call will be in grave danger? You've put us all in the line of fire."

"Would you prefer I let those boys get killed? Or leave those women as sex slaves? Where exactly did I go wrong?" I asked. She stared up at me through her clear eyelashes and I downed the rest of my rum, feeling the heat travel down my throat and land in my empty stomach, reaching out its tendrils of comfort. "Maybe it's time you were in the fucking line of fire, you cowardly bitch." I dropped the money on the desk and turned, grabbing the bottle of Old Monk and taking it with me.

I stepped out into the hall and walked over to the tinted glass, staring out into the street. Traffic flowed by - rickshaws, scooters, cars, but no vans. I put down the bottle of Old Monk on the industrial grey carpeting and sat next to it. I heard footsteps behind me and was surprised to see Chloe settle on the floor beside me, pulling up her skirt to sit cross-legged. "I got into this work because I cared. God, I cared so God damn much." She took off her glasses and placed them on the floor, then swiped at her eyes, brushing away tears. I picked up the bottle of Old Monk and refilled her glass. She went on, "Caring alone won't save them, though."

I nodded. "I'm counting on you."

She nodded and drank deeply from her glass, emptying it in one go. "I'll try," she said.

"Trying's not enough," I said. "Just fucking do it."

That's when I saw the van turn the corner and my heart leapt, knowing Dan was here and safe. Jumping to my feet I pulled the first door open, but the second was locked. Chloe pulled out her keys and opened it as the van pulled to a stop in front of the building. Chloe started to follow me out. "Don't you have phone calls to make?" I asked. "Doctor?"

She nodded. "Yes, you're right, I do. But, what will we do with them?"

"I think we should take them to the church."

Chloe glanced at her watch; it was thin and gold, delicate like the wrist it wrapped around. "The service should be over. Agapito will be there. I'll call and let him know you're coming."

"Good." I wet my lips. "I'm sorry about what I said."

Chloe nodded and a soft smile curled her lips. "I'm sorry I was being such a cowardly bitch."

Dan was out of the van, going around to open the door for his passengers when I reached him. His tan skin looked yellow in the street lights; dark circles under his eyes made him look almost sickly. The light that flowed from his pale green eyes felt like a fever. "The boy just ran," he said.

"It's okay, you saved his life."

He shook his head and then pulled open the sliding door. The two boys still clung to each other and the women seemed to all have linked arms. Every one of them seemed intertwined with another. And yet, none of them seemed comforted by the others. Maybe there was no comfort here. What could I do to help them, I wondered. My heart felt like it was getting tugged out of my chest.

Anita joined us and in a gentle tone spoke to them in Hindi and then in Gujarati.

"We're going to take them to the church," I told Dan. "Are you okay to drive?"

He frowned. "Of course." Dan reached out and brushed a hair off my cheek. "Don't worry about me, Sydney. I'm good."

I just nodded and climbed into the passenger seat. A spray of blood arched across it and I leaned forward to avoid touching it. The interior stank of sweat, the iron scent of drying blood, and a spicy aroma I couldn't identify. An orange figure of Ganesh, the elephant god, was glued to the dash, his expression serene. Dan pulled out and I opened my window, letting the smoky scent of the city blow my hair from my face and fill my nostrils. I stared at the light that passed through the bullet holes. I looked over at Dan's set jaw and wild eyes. This isn't what I wanted for him.

The ride was only a couple of minutes. Anita parked right behind us. Agapito was waiting for us by the gate. He came forward and opened my door for me. "Are you okay?" he asked. Then looking behind me at the women and children who cowered there, he gasped.

"Chloe didn't tell you?" I asked.

"She was unclear."

Anita opened the side door and reached in to help the youngest boy out. He retreated from her and the other boy kept a protective arm around him. "Where should we take them?" I asked as I climbed out.

Agapito stared at the boys, not answering. "Father," I said softly. He turned to me. "Where should we take them? Several are injured, the women."

He nodded. "Yes, sorry. Of course." He looked down at his hands for a moment and then glanced up and down the street, his eyes filling with urgency. "We must hurry. The infirmary."

"Lead the way," I said.

Anita gave up trying to get the boys out and turned to the women who flowed out of the van, keeping a physical connection. They looked like a group of school children keeping track of their buddies, but with less clothing and more bruises. They'd already gotten lost. Maybe Agapito could help them find their way back. Esha and her sister were the last off. They'd found a blanket to cover the abused girl. Her eyes were glassy and she looked as if the weight of her head might drag her to the ground.

Agapito's eyes sprung with tears when he saw her, his head shaking back and forth with regret. "Show them to the infirmary," I said.

"What about the children?" he asked, gesturing to the two boys who cowered in the front row.

"I'll try and get them out," I said. "Hurry."

Agapito nodded and then walked quickly down the stone path toward the church, his black frock making him disappear in the darkness. The women, in their tatters of dirty white robes and dresses, snaked behind him like a tail.

I turned to the boys in the van and crouched down. They stared at me with wide and frightened eyes that glinted in the darkness. Anita and Dan stood beside me. "Maybe we need to give them some more space," I said.

"I'm really worried about the van getting spotted," Anita said.

"Think there is parking around the back?" Dan asked.

I just watched the boys while they watched me. "Do you think they are afraid of me?"

"Probably," Anita said. "They did just watch you kill what? Like three people?"

"Tell them they are under my protection," I said.

Anita translated and the boys kept their eyes on me.

"Tell them that I will never let anyone hurt them again. That they can trust me."

I listened to Anita's translation and watched the boys. The braver of the two nodded his understanding and then lacing his fingers with the other boy came forward. I put a hand on his narrow shoulder and felt a surge of protectiveness that rushed adrenaline into my system. In that moment I wanted to fly over to Kalpesh Shah's house and shoot him so many times that his own uncle wouldn't recognize him when they met in Hell.

The boy looked up at me and I smiled. "You're safe now," I said. He took my hand and together we walked down the path to the church, leaving Anita and Dan to deal with the van.

The door was still open, and we stepped into the nave. The judgmental depiction of St. Nicholas was dark, but candles burned in sconces, lighting the pews and casting dancing shadows into the corners. The boys stopped in the door, hesitant to enter the strange space. I smiled. "I know," I said. "Totally weird, right?"

They didn't answer. I pulled on the braver boy's hand leading him down the aisle as his companion followed. Turning at the altar, I looked up at the plastic Jesus above the exit. The more fearful boy started crying and I turned to him, crouching down, and wiped his tears away. I felt my own chin wobble watching him struggle to understand what was happening, fear ripping him apart. "What's your name?" I asked. Pointing to myself, I said, "Sydney."

The braver boy pointed at his chest and answered, "Raju." When the smaller boy didn't answer he pointed at him and said, "Yash."

"Thank you, Raju," I said. "Yash..." I pursed my lips, knowing there was nothing I could say in any language that would stop his tears. Instead I reached out and picked the boy up. He wrapped his arms around me and cried onto my shoulder. I took Raju's hand and said, "Come on, boys. You're going to be okay. I promise." We passed under the mournful Jesus into the school.

Hearing voices I followed the sounds to an open door. I looked into the room and saw Agapito standing at a sink. The women were spread out over several beds, many still holding hands. The smell of antiseptic stung my nose. The priest looked up from the sink and, seeing me, nodded. "A doctor is on the way," he said. Agapito was holding a wet cloth, pink with diluted blood. Esha sat closest to him, her arm wrapped around her sister. She whispered softly to the girl.

"Perhaps you should help her," Agapito said. "I do not think she needs any more men touching her."

"Sure. I left Anita and Dan with the van. Is there somewhere they can park it out of sight?"

"Yes, yes," he nodded. "I'll show them."

I patted Yash's back and then placed him on the floor; he looked up at me, still crying. Raju took his hand. The boys stayed close to me as I crossed the room and took the cloth from Agapito. Esha smiled at me and said something to her sister that made the injured woman looked up at me. A small smile appeared on her cracked and swollen lips.

I reached out tentatively and touched the wet cloth to a patch of dried blood on the girl's face. She winced at my touch and I clucked the way my mother used to when she bandaged my booboos. "You'll be okay," I said. As I cleaned the woman's face, wiping away the dirt and pus, I thought that I'd been doing a little too much of this. At least I could rest easy in the fact that the people who did this would never hurt anyone else. But I also knew that didn't mean this girl would be okay or that there was any security for any of the victims in this room.

Chloe arrived with a man in his late fifties, he had Henna-tinted white hair and carried an old fashioned doctor's bag. The man had gentle eyes and moved to Esha's side speaking softly. She nodded at his questions. I stepped back and dropped the cloth into the sink. Agapito waited in the hall and motioned for me to join him. Yash and Raju followed me, slipping their hands into mine.

Agapito looked down at them and smiled, then turned his gaze to me, his eyes darkening. "Sydney, there is a lot of blood in the van."

"I know, we've got to clean it up soon or it will only get harder."

He frowned. "What happened?"

"Not sure you want to know, Father."

He pursed his lips and looked down at the boys. "I'm glad that they are safe."

"Good, let's leave it at that."

Agapito looked back up at me. "I cannot condone violence, no matter who it is against."

I looked up at the ceiling composing myself. "Got it. Look," I breathed deeply calming my tone so as not to frighten the boys. "I told you our methods differed. I'm not turning the other cheek."

"Yes, but Sydney. Murder?"

"Murder? I guess that's one way of looking at it. I think of it as defending the innocent. It's not like I just went out and shot some random people on the street." Agapito opened his mouth to speak, but I cut him off. "You've tried for years to save the kids Kalpesh has been abusing." I shook my head. "And you failed because you're not willing to get your hands dirty."

"Yes, Sydney, that's right. You are dirtying yourself. Lowering yourself to his level."

"No," I heard my voice rising and felt Raju squeeze my hand. I paused and looked down at him, smiling. "It's okay," I said and nodded. Turning back to Agapito I continued, keeping my voice even. "I am not lowering myself to any level. I am helping. You're the one who is hiding in this church, afraid to do anything that might actually make a difference."

Agapito's face reddened. "We make a difference here."

"Not enough of one," I spat at him, sick to death of this conversation. "Stop moralizing at me. It's because of my actions that these boys are alive and those women are free."

Chloe spoke behind me. "Yes, but how long will they stay alive? Kalpesh will come for them, for all of us."

I turned to her. "Not if I get to him first."

"Will you?" Agapito asked. "And what will you do then? Murder him?"

I shook my head. "I told you my plans for him."

"I guess you've left us no choice," Chloe said, looking over her shoulder at the women in the infirmary.

"You can throw us all out," I said.

Agapito put his hands up. "Let's just drop this. We have come too far to go back now. I pray that you are right, Sydney."

"I am," I said, holding his gaze.

He laid his hand on my shoulder and squeezed. "Your faith is admirable."

"As is yours, Father."

"Come," he said to the boys. Crouching down to them, he pulled several colored pencils from within his robes. "Shall we go draw?" He mimicked the action of sketching.

"I think they are Nepalese," Chloe said. "Many of them are." I let go of their hands and pushed them toward the priest who led them down the hall toward the art room.

"We've got to keep moving," I said to Chloe. "The van needs to be cleaned and hidden."

"You can leave it here," she said.

"Perfect, we can use it when we rescue the rest of the kids."

She nodded and then silently led me out into the play yard past the still swings and empty slide to a door in the wall. It led to a small parking area concealed from the road by bushes. Not the most secure spot in the world but it would have to do, I figured.

Dan and Anita waited by the van. "We need sponges and stuff," Dan said.

Chloe nodded. "Come with me." Anita started for the church and Dan went to follow, but I grabbed his hand, holding him back. He turned to look at me and I reached up touching his cheek. "I know this isn't what you signed up for," I said.

He shook his head. "This is exactly what I signed up for; I told you I'd go anywhere with you and I wasn't lying." The devotion in his eyes took my breath away in a wash of emotions. Fear and pride rolled over me.

"Come on." He held onto my hand as we headed inside. Chloe gave us a bucket of soapy water and several sponges. Looking over at Dan and Anita as we opened the van door and got to work, I felt a pang of uncertainty. I didn't want either of them to know what it was like to clean blood out of seat cushions, but here they were learning it. Anita threw up, running across the pavement and making it to the bushes before retching up yellow bile, the only thing left in her stomach. But Dan just clenched his jaw tighter and scrubbed with me until we'd done all we could. We'd never get the smell out, but it was better.

Exhausted and disgusted, I went back into the church and looked into the art room. Agapito sat with the boys, paper and pencils around them. I leaned against the doorjamb and smiled, feeling that if nothing else these boys were having this moment. Maybe they would grow up to be men like Agapito, doing as much good as they knew how. What more could we ask for in this world?

We took two rickshaws back to Anita's place, getting dropped off blocks away and then trudging the final distance. The moon was setting and the stars were gone. Two cows slept next to Anita's door, a mother with her calf curled up beside her. The tender way in which they lay made my breath catch in my throat.

CHAPTER SIXTEEN
COMING UP WITH A PLAN

When I woke up the next morning, I felt like I had a terrible hangover. My whole body ached and my head pounded. Blue whined and licked my face. I pushed him away and groaned. Dan was awake, staring up at the ceiling.

My teeth felt like they were wearing socks. I needed a run. Reaching for the ceiling I stretched my back. Blue wagged his tail and then with a yowl stretched his back too, pushing his tail high into the air.

I pulled on my jogging shorts, sports bra, and a T-shirt. Dan watched me, plucking at a pillow. "You okay?" I asked, looking up from tying my running shoes.

He smiled at me. "Sure."

"Want to come for a run?"

He laughed. "I think I'll just smoke a joint instead."

I smiled. "Sounds good."

Blue followed me down the steps. We found Anita in the kitchen. She was wearing a light cotton bathrobe, block printed with a pattern of green dragons, heads arched back, tongues extended. Her hair was wet and her eyes still puffy from sleep. "Sydney," she said, looking up from her phone, "they're moving the children."

"What?"

"The kids, Kalpesh is moving them again."

She refilled her coffee cup, gesturing toward the pot, asking if I wanted a cup. "After my run," I said.

"I don't know if that's a good idea."

My body felt tight, and I knew that I'd think a lot better if I got the chance to run it loose. And Blue might just explode if I didn't get him some exercise. Blue understood that he'd missed some serious action last night and it made him antsy. "I really need a run," I said.

"Sydney, after what happened last night?" she shook her head. "It's not as if you blend in around here."

"I'll take my chances."

Her eyes narrowed. "It's not just *your chances* that you're taking. They're mine, too, and Dan's."

I pursed my lips, hating the reminder. At least I didn't have to worry about Anita writing this story anymore. It was a good thing she felt that we were intertwined. Anita poured another cup of coffee and placed it on the table. "We need to strategize. Our position has become much more precarious, not to mention Chloe's and Agapito's."

I sat down at the table and Blue looked at me like I was a traitor. "I at least need to take him for a pee," I said.

"Fine," Anita turned back to her phone.

Blue pranced next to me as I pulled open the ancient door. The street was empty, the cows from the night before gone. I walked slowly down the alley letting Blue sniff. He did his business and I started back toward the house. Looking up and down the empty block one more time, I picked up my pace, then digging my toes in, I sprinted past the door. Blue flew next to me, his long legs extending. Reaching the end of the block I skidded and turned, racing back the other way. Blue jumped up and touched his nose to my elbow letting me know how much fun he thought this was. Five more sprints and my lungs threatened to give out. Blue panted heavily as we reentered the house and sweat spotted my T-shirt.

Dan sat at the kitchen table, a joint in one hand, a cup of coffee in the other. He smiled at me and I smiled back. Dan looked okay, tired, but not devastated. The rich smell of hash filled the room. Anita came down the steps dressed in linen pants and a button-down white shirt. She took in my sweaty appearance and frowned.

"I just ran up and down the street for a minute. No one saw me," I said. Blue went over to his bowl of water and lapped at it thirstily.

Anita pulled out her phone and sat at the table. "We have a bunch to go over." Dan offered her the joint and she shook her head. "I don't understand you two," she said, her voice rising. "Why aren't you freaking out!"

Dan and I made eye contact and then turned to Anita. "We've done this before," I said.

"You just seem so goddamn calm."

"I'm not that calm," Dan said, taking another drag off the joint.

I was calm. Utterly calm. The best way to be in a situation like this. The only time I felt so at peace.

"We don't even have a plan," Anita said, throwing up her hands. "We are so lucky that last night turned out the way it did. We all could have died. And those kids..."

"Yes, we all could have died," I said, putting food in a bowl for Blue. He sat before I asked and then flopped into the down position. "But we didn't, so that feels good, right?"

Anita stared at me as I put Blue through a couple of commands before telling him to eat, which he did with gusto. I looked back over at Anita. "What do we know about his security?"

Anita squeezed her eyes shut and didn't answer. "From the research I've done," Dan said, opening his laptop, "he's not that high tech. I found a basic alarm system and some video, but not enough. If I was setting up this guy's system, I'd be a lot more into surveillance." He put the joint out into his empty coffee cup with a sizzle.

"Are we still thinking of taking him at the Kite Festival?" I asked. "That's in two days."

"Any chance we can get into his place before that?" Dan asked. "I'd love to place a couple of cameras. That would make our attack a lot easier. I could basically be in the van letting you know where his people were. How many guards does he have again?" Dan asked, turning to Anita.

"What about the fact that we don't actually know where the kids are," Anita held up one finger, "he has fifteen guards," another finger popped up, "and the entire city is on his side?"

I shook my head. "First of all, I don't think the city is really on his side. They're just not doing anything to stop him. That's out of fear or greed, not because they agree with what he is doing. Secondly, can't your source tell us where the kids are? And the guards, I'd say that's a real honest-to-God problem. You've got me there. Dan, any ideas?"

He pursed his lips thinking.

Anita flicked at her phone. "My source can probably locate the children."

"I'd like to talk to him or at least know who he is at this point."

"I've asked if he'd be willing to speak with you, but not yet."

"We've got two days," I said.

"There is a party tonight, it's invitation only but we can get in. My source will decide then if he trusts you."

I filled a glass with water and sat down at the table. "Fine," I said. "But I still think taking him at the Kite Festival makes sense because he has to let us in to his big open-house celebration. And there will be a lot of people around, so it's easy to blend."

"But I think we need to get the kids out before we take him," Dan said. "Because otherwise they are basically dead."

"I agree."

"We should go to the kite market tonight," Anita said.

I shrugged. "Why?"

"We will run into Shah and then he'll have to invite me to his party afterwards."

"Really? Even though his henchmen tried to rape and kill you?"

"I've known him my whole life. If he didn't invite me it would be a clear indication that it was his men, that he was behind the attack. Shah must pretend like everything is normal. That's what this game is all about, don't you see? If we don't expose him, it will be as if none of this ever happened."

"If you're going to the kite market I'll go pick up some surveillance cameras," Dan said. "That way we can put some around, at least in the public areas."

"Sounds like a plan," I said, standing up and heading for a shower.

CHAPTER SEVENTEEN
THE KITE MARKET

Pedestrian traffic thickened as we approached the market. Young men, thin and lithe, smiled and hung their arms around each other in groups of three or four. We reached the top of the street and I looked into the mayhem. The road was teeming with cows, rickshaws, motorcycles, dogs, anything and everything. Vehicles moved back and forth through the sea of people, standing out as islands. Drawn by stalls filled with kites, masks, hats, and glass-coated string, people clung to the edges like leaves pushed out of a stream and onto the shore.

Some of the kites were just simple colored paper, cocktail napkins for the sky. Others had geometric designs and tails that promised to flutter in the wind. Some featured well-known Disney characters and were made from materials that would stink when burned. "There will be hundreds of people," Anita said to me over my shoulder as we maneuvered through the crowd. "All of these people here, tomorrow will be on their roofs, flying kites."

The tables filled the stalls so that the sellers sat on them along with their wares. Women in bright saris with bored expressions on their faces looked out at the crowd; men of all ages smiled at me. The glass-laced string, bright pink wrapped around wooden spools, was sold at every stall. What would a kite be without its weapon?

Standing next to Anita as she haggled with a merchant, I spied a pile of zip ties in the corner. I plucked at Anita's sleeve. She ignored me at first, deep into her bargaining, but I tugged more persistently. Finally, she turned to me. "What?"

"Get some of those zip ties." She looked where I was pointing and then showed them to the young man she was negotiating with. He pulled out several and showed Anita their strength. She looked unimpressed but agreed upon his price and handed over a small bundle of rupees.

As the sun began to set the women left and the men's voices became more boisterous, their groups larger, and their smiles turned to leers. Anita said that even though we hadn't found Kalpesh, we should go.

Before I could respond, I felt a disturbance in the crowd, a parting of the sea, and then he was in front of us. I recognized him from the pictures Dan showed me. In the images he was almost always at an "event" with his nose tilted down at the camera, a glass held close to his chest. His fingers were decorated with gold rings set with cartoon-size jewels. The scar that ran down the side of his face would have looked fake, still so fresh after all these years, except that it pulled on the skin of his right eye, distorting his features ever so slightly.

There was a pudginess about him that spoke of too much booze and rich food, but not so little activity that he became truly fat. He probably does a lot of coke. And the way he was sweating, even in the shade of the umbrella that one of his security men held over him, it seemed not so much from the heat of the waning day but from something inside him.

There were four bodyguards with him. Three large men and one small. The little man only reached as high as my neck but his strong compact body, penetrating gaze, and Bruce Lee haircut made me think he might be the most badass among them. He and one of the behemoths stepped to Kalpesh's sides, forming a break in the crowd, forcing themselves into a menacing semi-circle around us. Within Kalpesh Shah's sphere there was no jostling.

"Anita, my dear, what a pleasure to see you," he said, then licked his top lip, sucking off some of the moisture that lingered there. "My goodness," Kalpesh continued, raising a manicured hand to his mouth in a show of shock, "what happened to your face?" He reached out to touch Anita, but she jerked away. Her lips trembled.

"You look frightened my dear, is it the crowds? So much can happen in a crowd." He looked around at the men streaming past, their eyes gliding over our bodies. "I understand your fears. Would you like an escort back to your house?"

When Anita didn't answer he rested his heavy lidded eyes on me, and there was nothing coming out of them. It was like looking into a reflecting pool on a moonless night. Blackness, with just the breeze playing hints of movement along the surface.

"You are quite lovely," he said to me. His teeth flashed white and slimy. "Even with those scars on your face." He rocked back on his heels. "Tell me, how did you get yours?"

I didn't answer him right away, taking another moment to try to find some humanity in his eyes. A cow meandered by— people, vehicles, everything pouring around it; the velvet-clad boulder of the Ahmedabad street stream. It passed closely, a group of flies orbiting it. The animal's tail flicked out and almost touched Kalpesh's shoulder, but the little bodyguard held up a hand for it to pat against instead.

"I imagine in a similar manner to how you got yours," I finally answered.

"Ah, so you know how I got mine?"

"Most come from the same place."

He leaned back and looked further down his nose at me. "Scars on your face tell a specific story?" he asked. I shrugged, not breaking eye contact. "Perhaps," he said smiling, suddenly delighted. "They show that you are brave, foolish, and still alive." He swiveled his head to rest his gaze on Anita. "Until, of course," he laughed, "you're dead." He laughed at his own joke, his henchmen joined, their shoulders shaking up and down rhythmically with his. He was the first to stop and the rest ended their guffaws instantly.

"Yes," I said. "They remind me."

"Remind you of what?" he asked, not taking his eyes off of Anita.

"Of how unfair the world is."

"Why do you want to be reminded of that?" He wrinkled his nose and chuckled, casting his glance back to me.

"It's not that I want to, it's just what happens when I look at my scars."

"They remind you of injustice, unfairness?" He smiled slickly, oily, slippery. He had not survived this long by being stupid or clumsy. But he was certainly arrogant. He did not fear anyone. Especially not a woman.

Standing in the eddy that his security created, I got a taste of the world Shah lived in, protected and confused. No one ever says no to him, I thought. He is a creature, created by his circumstances. What would this man be like if he'd been born into the jungle of the street life that so many Indians live?

Shah tilted his head, looking at me for a moment. And then turning to Anita said, "I must be going, but please, join us this evening." He turned back to me, "I host a small party every year at my ancestral home the night before Kite Festival The place is a masterpiece, you've never seen anything like it."

"I'm sure it's beautiful," I said.

"The party is just for family and friends." He smiled. "But I would be happy to host any friends of Anita's. Has she told you of me?" Without waiting for me to answer he continued. "No?" he asked, pitching his voice high and looking back at Anita. "But I seem to occupy her mind so very much, as she occupies mine." He played with the words in his mouth. His jaw was working, circling, biting, crunching; coked up, I thought, no way around it.

I couldn't stand the thought of his sweaty, bloated face pressing into young flesh. The images that flashed before my eyes filled me with revulsion. The crowd was suddenly too close, the smells of all those bodies forcing into my nose. Looking at Anita I could see she was having trouble maintaining her composure.

"Thank you so much for the generous offer and the invitation. I've been longing to see inside one of those wonderful old Ahmedabad homes." I smiled up at Kalpesh, trying to fill my eyes with wonder and innocence.

He looked down over puffy cheeks, his head held high, posing a regal angle, but he didn't look like royalty. I held his gaze, grinning gleefully, as he continued to scrutinize me. "I just can't wait," I said.

He let a small smile slip onto his lips. "Yes, my dear, it will be a magical evening. My ancestral home is more magnificent than you can possibly imagine."

"I'm sure," I said.

And then he left us there, his security team clearing a path for him through the crowd.

CHAPTER EIGHTEEN
THE PARTY

Dan was waiting for us when we got back to Anita's. We barely had time to change before the party. "I got the cameras," he said as soon as we walked in.

"Great, we got the invite," I said.

Dan grinned.

"We better get dressed," Anita said, hurrying up the stairs. "The party starts in an hour."

With taking Blue out, changing, and the short walk to Kalpesh's house, we arrived a half hour late. Dan wore a suit we'd bought in Mumbai that fit him nicely, and with a fresh shave the man looked downright presentable. My kurta was a deep red and hemmed with bright orange silk embroidery. Anita had thought to wear a Sari, but I'd convinced her she might want pants so she'd picked a silk kurta that appeared bright blue in some lights, and lavender in others.

The whole alleyway leading to the entrance was strung in bright blue lights, the color that might surround an evil witch while she burned. The gate to the garden was propped open, and a man waited with a tray of glasses bubbling with champagne.

"Gujurat is a dry state for some, a very wet one for others," Anita whispered to me as I took a glass with a nod and a thank you.

"I don't know if you should drink that," Dan said. "It might be drugged. Remember the choir."

I sniffed the glass and looked around at the crowd milling in the front courtyard. Glowing in the candlelight they looked beautiful. A woman in a night-blue sari woven with silver paisleys and gold trim laughed a soft tinkling sound. A tall man with short cropped hair and round glasses smiled at her.

They all looked so elegant, draped the way they were around the courtyard, under the bougainvillea that topped the boundary wall. On the veranda, men laughed and women tittered. Thrumming techno that did not match the scene blasted from a nearby building.

"They love this music but I tell you, I can't stand it," Kalpesh Shah said, gesturing to the sky and all those not at his party, as he approached us. "You found drinks, wonderful. Please come in, come in."

I gestured to Dan. "This is my boyfriend, Dan, I hope you don't mind that I brought him."

Kalpesh smiled and let his eyes slowly wander up and down Dan's body. He looked like he appreciated the way Dan's suit fit just as much as I did. "Not at all," Kalpesh said. "Please," he smiled. "You're all welcome."

We stepped further into the compound and up the steps into the house. A row of stone, squatting Buddhas held candles that flickered in the overhead fan's breeze. "Are you hungry?" Kalpesh asked. He waved at a waiter cruising by with a tray of samosas. The young man changed course and offered the hors d'oeuvre to the master of the house.

Among the elegantly dressed, I spied Kalpesh's security, mostly large men in black suits that fit them perfectly. If it weren't for their watchful eyes and contained manner I wouldn't have been able to tell them from the guests. Kalpesh saw my eyes. "I have them made," he said.

"Excuse me?"

"The suits," he said. "You were admiring the men's suits. I have them made for them. It's important that a suit fits."

Kalpesh did not wear a suit himself. A purple kurta of the finest silk draped over his round belly and ended below his knees. Shah reached out and took a samosa off the tray; he bit into it and surveyed the room, perhaps looking for someone more important or interesting to talk to. His jaw was working the samosa like it was saw dust. He sucked down some of his champagne. The young man looked at me, but I waved off the fried treats. Kalpesh had a way of making everything look unappetizing.

But the house was indeed gorgeous. The pillars holding up the ancient building were carved with intricate patterns. Antique furniture filled the space and well-groomed guests, in turn, filled the furniture. Shah beckoned me on through another doorway and into an interior courtyard.

Craning his neck to look up to the dark sky he said, "Are you looking forward to your first Kite Festival?"

"I am," I said. The courtyard was filled with people smoking and laughing. The bar was set into one corner and a large man bellowed from next to it, his face turning red with hilarity. "Isn't it dangerous?" I asked.

Shah lowered his gaze and smiled at me. "Yes," he said. "It is very dangerous."

A woman stumbled and fell into Kalpesh. He bounced into me and I felt his bulk. Bile rose in my throat as I quickly moved away from him, knocking into Anita. Dan's hand came out and squeezed my elbow. I caught his eye and he smiled at me, silently telling me to relax. That everything was cool.

After apologizing for bumping into us, the woman grabbed Kalpesh's arm and dragged him away into the crowd. Anita moved deeper into the house with Dan and I following her. She dropped her empty glass onto a waiter's tray as he passed. Moving to the bar she got in line, then ordered a gin and tonic.

I still had plenty of champagne, but Dan got a beer. We stood off to the side sipping our drinks and surveying the crowd. We were not the only Westerners there. I saw a woman with red hair and pale white skin who looked doped up and boneless, flopping around on a couch with a man twenty years her senior by her side, ignoring her. I saw a young man, probably not even eighteen, holding a whiskey and talking with

Shah. The boy recoiled slightly when Kalpesh reached out and stroked his cheek, but he didn't run away.

"Bloody good to see another of my kind here," a large man said, slapping Dan on the back. He was British, big, red-faced, and guessing from the way his eyes rolled in their sockets, five to seven drinks ahead of us. Dan didn't know how to respond but that worked fine for this guy. "You ever see this kind of a thing before?" he asked, then answered, "It's my first time at a shindig of this caliber, over here at least. Just got here three days ago and already I'm dining at the Shah's." He laughed loudly and slapped Dan again, who rocked forward a little from the blow. "You here on business?" he asked, and then answered, "I'm a salesman, medical stuff mostly. The doctor I'm working with over at the hospital," he gestured off to the side—I'm not sure if he meant to be pointing at the doctor or the hospital but either way a little of his drink spilled over the edge of his glass and splattered onto the floor without him noticing —"he invited me to this and, boy, am I glad he did." The man laughed again, rocking back on his heels and bringing his glass into his belly. "And here I was thinking that I wouldn't be able to get a drink over here."

I reached my hand into my pocket and felt the small cameras there. Each of us carried three, with instructions to put them someplace smart. Dan leapt out of the way right as the big guy went to slap him again. The Brit hardly noticed and just kept talking. Anita took my arm and said, "We're going to the ladies' room."

Dan looked at us like an abandoned puppy, while his captor kept up his steady stream of nonsense. Anita guided me through the crowd further into the house. We left the courtyard and entered a smaller room where several men sat huddled together, cigar smoke swirling around them, talking in hushed voices.

"Deals are always being made," she said, once we'd passed them. There was a small line at the bathroom, and we waited in silence with two other women who both had their heads bent over their phones.

When it was Anita's turn she pulled me into the small space with her. "Where do you think we should put the cameras?" she whispered.

"One on the steps leading up to the roof so that we can see how much security is going up and down, one on or near the front door so we can see who comes and goes, one in the alley." I bit my lip thinking. "It's a shame we can't get into the rest of the house, but he's got men on every exit."

Anita nodded. "Yes, I think the children will be held in one of the other buildings, but we won't know until we find them."

The man's property spanned blocks, and he had buildings all over the city. What if he was keeping them somewhere else? Taking a deep breath, I calmed my worries.

"I'll go and plant the one on the steps and the one by the front door," Anita said. "We can do the alley on our way out. You and Dan can go exploring, looking for more spots. If anyone questions you, Dan can pretend like he was trying to get you alone."

"Sounds good," I said.

I found Dan right where I'd left him. His eyes lit up when he spotted me moving through the crowd. Anita veered off and began chatting with a group on one of the couches. I took Dan's arm and said to the Brit, "I've got to steal him away for a moment."

The big man smiled and nodded, but didn't break his commentary, he just turned and started laying it on the unsuspecting guy next to him. "Thank you," Dan said. "I didn't know you could be bored while infiltrating a madman's lair, but it turns out the British are still coming up with new forms of torture."

"Want to go find a place to make out?" I asked.

Dan laughed. "What?"

I steered him toward the steps to the upper levels of the courtyard. "Anita's idea," I said. "Make like we're real hot for each other and try to get into the rest of the house."

"Yes, Captain," he said.

I slapped him playfully on the arm before pushing him in front of me to climb the steps. Another flight continued up onto the roof and one of Kalpesh's well-groomed bodyguards waited at the bottom. "Not tonight," he said, as Dan opened his mouth. "Tomorrow. Come back tomorrow, and you can go on the roof."

Dan smiled. "Sure." He stepped closer to the man. They were about the same height but Dan's shoulders were not as broad, his forehead not so short, and his eyes not so hard. Dan cleared his throat. "I'm looking for a private place." He tilted his head toward me. "Someplace quiet."

The man's eyes flicked to me for a second and then went back to Dan. "Not on the roof."

"Fair enough," Dan said, stepping back. "We'll just take a stroll then."

The guard didn't answer, and we moved around the railing. It was a fifteen foot drop to the bar and crowd below. I saw Kalpesh talking a mile a minute to a group of young men who all nodded their heads in eager approval of the older man's words. Another couple passed us with eyes only for each other, the man's arm slung across the woman's narrow shoulders. Dan wrapped his arm around my waist and rested his hand on my hip bone, pulling me close to him.

We circled the upstairs and then turned to head back. There were doors along our walk and I tried the first one. It was unlocked and led to another bathroom. "Someone should tell the ladies downstairs about this one," I said.

Dan tried the next door and, finding it locked, moved on. I tracked Kalpesh as he moved through the crowd beneath us, a young man trailing after him. They climbed the steps and, reaching our level, turned toward us. I pulled Dan into a dark corner and he followed me easily, facing his back to Kalpesh. I peeked around Dan's shoulder and watched as Kalpesh and the young man passed the guard and went down the corridor to a door we had not tried yet. Kalpesh called the guard over and told him to unlock it.

Leaving the staircase to the roof unattended, the bodyguard pulled out a set of keys and unlocked the door for them. They went through, and the guard did not re-lock the door before returning to the staircase. The guard's eyes wandered toward us and I quickly tilted my face up and kissed Dan. Not one to leave a girl hanging, Dan reciprocated, making our fake make-out session into a reality. Dan came up for air and smiled down at me. "How'm I doing?"

"Great," I said. "Come with me."

I took Dan's hand and led him over to the door Shah went through. I pressed him against the wall near it and kissed at his neck. "Try the handle," I whispered. "But make sure the guard isn't looking." Dan's hand wandered from my waist down to my butt. "That's not the door handle," I said.

Dan pushed off the wall and flipped us, leaning me against it, right next to the doorjamb. "That guy wasn't taking his eyes off us with you in the front," he said, leaning into my hair, flicking his tongue at my ear. I felt heat rush to my face and other parts. His hand left my hip and felt for the knob. "Unlocked, I think," Dan said, his voice husky.

Faux making out felt a lot like the real thing, I thought, as Dan's hand came back to my waist. "How are we going to get through there?" I said.

"We have to distract the guy," Dan said, and then returned to his duty as ardent lover. I tried to think about that, but Dan was doing a hell of a job distracting me.

I was about to push him away to try to get the fog out of my mind when a crash from below startled us. The guard hurried down a couple of steps. Dan started to head toward the railing to see what happened, but I opened the door behind us and pulled him in after me.

There was a long corridor in front of us that ended in a T. We started down the hall on tiptoes, listening. It didn't take long to hear the thumping of wood, the grunting of men, and the small cries of pleasure —or was that pain? We stopped outside a door that stood slightly ajar. Peering in I saw Shah's naked back. Sweat trickled down his spine. The man's skin looked blanched, like something rotten that had been boiled in a failed attempt to make it palatable. I couldn't see the young man under him except for a hand that clutched the desk's edge. The room was an office. Taking one of the cameras out of my pocket I curled a finger around the open door and pressed the sticky side onto the jamb.

We continued down the hall. As we reached the end, noises from the two men became louder, the thumping more insistent and then with a heavy sigh, a soft cry, the sounds stopped. We ducked left and tried the first door. It was unlocked and the room we stepped into was pitch black once the door closed behind us.

We waited in the darkness, our ears straining to hear the outer door close behind Shah and his young lover. I took long deep breaths trying to slow my heart rate. Dan reached out and laced his fingers through mine, a loving and chaste move.

In time we heard footsteps and low voices. What we both agreed sounded like the outer door opening and closing followed. Waiting another beat I opened our door and listened. I heard the lock turn on our exit. Shit.

My feet hardly made a sound as I padded down the hallway, Dan behind me, his hand linked with mine. The door was indeed locked. Without a sound I steered us back down to the T, but Dan pulled me toward the room Shah had left. He pushed open the door and pulled me in. The room was dark and smelled like sex and computers. Dan closed the door behind us, then flicked on a light.

An office was revealed—wooden filing cabinets, a couch, and three desks all with computers on them. The one I'd seen Kalpesh humping on looked disturbed, but only slightly. A couple of pages of paper were littered on the floor and the lamp was askew.

Dan looked at the computers and smiled. "What?" I asked.

"Maybe there are records on these bad boys. Maybe we can get some of these kids back to their families."

"Didn't their families sell them?" I asked.

"Not all of them," came a soft voice behind me. I whirled around, but didn't see anyone. Dan stepped close behind me.

"Hello?" I said.

He unfolded himself from between two filing cabinets. It was the little bodyguard from the Kite Market. He wore the fitted black suit and stern face of the rest of Kalpesh's body guards, but this guy was obviously different. He moved like something out of a dream, completely fluid, never off-weight, never weak, always ready.

I tensed, unsure of how this was going to go. He didn't seem on the verge of attacking me. Hell, he could have killed me while my back was turned. Nor did the little man seem worried about me attacking him, though he kept his eyes on me as he moved toward us. "You won't find the records on the computers," he said. He cocked his head, listening. "We must go." The little guy reached his hand out to me. When I didn't take it, he said, "I know Anita." He turned and listened again. "Please," he said, turning back to me.

I took his hand, Dan took mine, and we followed the small man out a side door. He hurried us along an exterior hallway, big windows looked out onto the street. At the last one he pushed aside the curtains, flung open the window, and gestured for me to jump. I heard commotion behind us. "They know you are missing. Quickly."

I leaned over the edge and saw a balcony ten feet below. We were in a corner of the building but there were no drainpipes around. I didn't know how he expected us to get down there without breaking a leg. Seeing my look of concern the bodyguard vaulted over the edge and, using the corner of the two buildings, bounced from one side to the other until alighting silently onto the balcony below.

The sounds of doors opening and closing behind us urged me forward. Better not to be tentative, I thought. Slipping out of my leather sandals I dropped them down to the balcony and following the small man's moves vaulted myself hard over the edge against the other building. I hit it like a spider and immediately pushed off, launching myself at the other wall, feet and palms out, ready to push off. One more and I found myself on the balcony, knees bent, still alive.

Dan looked down at me, forlorn. I beckoned for him to follow as I slipped back into my shoes but Dan didn't train like me. The guy did some pushups, crunches, and the occasional laps in the pool. He could not bound off walls. He looked over his shoulder and realizing he had no other choice, lowered himself out the window. With his arms fully extended he was less than three feet from the balcony.

"Bend your knees," I said as he let go, landing hard on the balcony with us. Before Dan even had a moment to enjoy his escape the little guy was moving again. He opened up the balcony doors and we walked back inside. This was a different building, I realized quickly as we crossed dusty, rotting wooden floors. Only one fluorescent bulb lit the hall, showing off peeling paint and dark corners.

The guard turned again, opened a door and led us through a large, dark, and, as far as I could tell by the echo of our feet, empty room. He crouched down and motioned for us to follow. I dropped into a squat, my eyes straining in the darkness to find the danger he sensed. After a moment he stood and continued without explanation.

We climbed a set of stairs, followed another dirty hallway to its end, where the little guy opened another window. A rickety wooden ladder led past dark windows to the roof where the moon powered through the city's light pollution, a fat, low-slung crescent of white.

As we moved across the metal roof the guard stopped and held his finger to his lips, pointing down to Dan's feet. "Sorry, but I'm not a..." Dan pursed his lips looking for the right word.

"A ninja," I whispered. "You're not a ninja."

"Exactly," Dan whispered. But the little guy was already moving across the roof again. He jumped a short distance onto another roof and then slowed, padding over to the opening of an interior courtyard.

He waved us over and we crouched next to him. Leaning over the edge I looked down onto a nursery. Single, child-size beds lined the courtyard; kids ranging in age from toddlers to early puberty sat around, probably a dozen or more. They didn't make any noise. No talking, no laughing, no playing. It was like looking down onto an art installation; wax children at play.

"You will help us?" I asked the small man at my side as I placed a camera on the roof's edge, aiming down at the children.

He turned to me, "I believe it is you who are here to help me," he answered. Motion below drew our attention as black-suited men entered the space, moving through it, looking for something. The small man backed away from the edge, Dan and I followed him across the roof and down the rickety wooden ladder. He motioned to the street below and then jumped, bouncing off a wall to the ground.

"Guy ever heard of steps?" Dan asked. I shrugged and followed the little guy, landing next to him in the narrow alleyway. Dan clung to the last rung of the ladder, stretching out his full height, dropping the final few feet and stumbling forward, catching himself with his palms.

Standing up he wiped his hands on his suite pants leaving streaks of brown dust. Dan looked around. "Just wide enough for the van. But we will need a ladder," he said.

"No," the guard said. He pointed to a metal, reinforced door down the street. "We bring them out there."

"How?" I asked. The little man pitched his head to the side again and then said he had to go. "Go straight home now."

"But Anita—"

"Go now." He made eye contact and held it. "Do not wait for her. This is important."

"Wait," I said, but he was already back up at the window. He didn't look down at us before disappearing inside.

Dan and I stood for a moment staring up at the empty window. "So that's Anita's source," Dan said.

"Yeah," I said. "But I don't think we should leave without Anita."

"Seems clear he's on her side. And it sounds like they are onto us. By staying we may be endangering her."

I bit my lip. "I guess you're right."

We placed cameras in the alley and then after circling around, managed to find Anita's house.

CHAPTER NINETEEN
WHAT MORE CAN I DO?

We sat at the kitchen table with a bottle of Old Monk rum between us. Dan and I drank in silence waiting for Anita. After my first glass I stood up and began to pace. "This isn't good," I said. "She's not back yet."

Dan nodded and refilled his glass. "Did we make a mistake trusting that man?"

I sipped at my rum, the taste reminded me of maple syrup, of childhood, of innocence.

"I think we can trust him," I said.

"Why?" Dan asked.

"Just do, don't know why." I put down my glass and stretched my arms over my head, feeling tight muscles rebelling against me. Blue growled at the stairs and then barked, his hackles rising high on his back. I bent my knees and raised my hands facing the darkness. The small guard stepped out of the shadows. "Okay, Blue," I said. He stopped barking, but a growl still rumbled in his chest.

When Dan stood, surprised by our visitor, he looked like a giant. The guard's posture was rigid, but his legs loose. I bet he was almost impossible to knock over. I didn't want to fight him, but I wanted to see him fight. I wanted to see him go crazy on someone. I knew he could bounce off walls; I bet he could fly through the air like an animal, a panther as much as a man.

I said, "Hello."

"Hello," he replied.

His voice was soft, the opposite of his hard physique. He looked like he was carved from a single piece of wood.

"I am Mana," he said.

"Sydney," I said, pointing to myself, "and this is Dan."

"You are here to help with the children," he said. "I appreciate your kinship."

Kinship, I thought. I wasn't sure that's what we were offering. But I liked the way it sounded from his mouth.

Mana's black hair hung almost to his shoulders, covering his ears. Short bangs stayed out of his eyes. He had broad cheekbones, a flat nose, and dark eyes that were penetrating, bright, like black quartz in a sunlit cave.

"Anita," he said. "Kalpesh is holding her."

"What do you mean 'holding her?'" Dan asked.

"She is his prisoner."

"Prisoner?" I said, my heart beating faster.

"I could not help now. But tomorrow. Tomorrow we will help her and free the children."

"She said that wouldn't happen. That he had to pretend everything was normal." I looked over at Dan. "I never would have, we never should have—" I turned back to Mana. "We should go now." I looked around the kitchen thinking about what I needed.

"Tomorrow is the day," he said.

"We can't leave her there overnight," I said. "God only knows what they will do to her."

"You and she will die if you go now."

"You don't know me," I said.

"I see that you are a very brave warrior, but there are too many men. You will not survive."

"I can't just leave her there," I said, hearing my voice raise into almost

144

a screech. Breathing in through my nose and out my mouth, I tried to calm down, to think about how to do this.

"She will suffer, yes," Mana said. "But not so much that she will not live."

I stared at him. Dan came to my side. "What's your plan?" he asked Mana.

"Tomorrow at ten a.m. the guests will begin to arrive. At noon lunch will begin to be served. Three seatings of no less than twenty, no more than forty. At four the chai will be served. I will put sleeping powder in the guards' tea so that at sunset when the fireworks begin, the guards will sleep. All except two. Me and Mugloo."

"Mugloo?" Dan asked.

"He is called the Bulldog," Mana said. "He only drinks from the water at his hip, trusts no one."

"Why are you doing this?" I asked.

"My brother," Mana said. "Kalpesh bought my brother. Now he has arrived, and I will take him."

"What? I don't understand. How did he get your brother?"

Mana's's face tightened. "I left my village five years ago to work and send money to my family. My father is," his jaw clenched before he continued. "he was desperate."

"Your father sold him?"

"Yes."

"But how do you know he is coming to Kalpesh? How did you trace him?" I asked.

His eyes met mine. "The work I did when I left my village was not honest, but it was not this." He sneered, and I saw strong emotions rise in his eyes, but he quickly brought himself back under control. "I started working for Kalpesh as soon as I found out where my brother was going. Safer to wait then to track."

"How long have you waited?" I asked.

"Five weeks," he answered. "I hope that you can wait one day."

"We have a van to get the kids out," Dan said. "Can you open the door?"

"Yes, but I will take my brother myself."

Dan nodded.

"Wait," I said, stepping back. Blue stayed close to me. "Are you okay with leaving Anita there?" I asked Dan.

He shook his head. "Of course not, but I don't think we can get her out now. We need Mana's help."

"But they will rape her!" I yelled.

Dan paled. "What can we do?"

I grabbed my leather jacket off the back of my chair and headed for the door, Blue stayed with me.

"Wait," Dan followed me. "Where are you going?"

"I'm going to get her."

Dan grabbed my arm. "You can't, we have to wait."

"Wait?" I spat at him. "Wait, for what, until they kill her?"

"No, no, if you go to get her now we won't be able to save the children or grab Kalpesh. And you'll probably get killed."

"I won't."

"Please, think about the bigger picture."

"I can't just sit here while she's being tortured or raped or whatever those sick fucks are doing. I am not waiting an entire day to save her."

"You have to."

I shook him off. "No, I don't."

Blue and I walked out the door, Dan following behind us. But as I strode down the block I realized I didn't have a plan. And I didn't have enough bullets. I stopped and clenched and unclenched my fists so hard that I left half-moon indentations in my palms. "Fuck!" I said.

Dan stood a couple of steps back. "Come inside. We'll come up with a plan, I promise."

"She is priority number one. Is that clear?"

"Yes, we will save her. But we can't do it until Mana knocks out the guards. There are too many."

I pictured Anita somewhere deep in the bowels of Shah's complex. How would I find her, I wondered with a shiver.

"Let's go back inside," Dan said, taking my elbow lightly.

I let him lead me into the house and watched as he poured me another shot of rum. "What about Shah?" I asked Mana who still stood by the dark stairwell. "We plan on taking him with us."

"You want to take him?" Mana asked.

"Yes, to France where he will be prosecuted."

"You can have him. I want my brother."

"It's important that the man faces justice," I said.

"I planned to kill him. Isn't that justice? His life for theirs."

"But he can be a symbol so that others will know not to try the same. That they can't get away with it."

The little man studied me for a moment. "Your gods and mine see things differently. If you want him you can have him. For my brother's freedom, and for Anita, that is why I fight. As long as you promise me justice."

I nodded. "Yes."

"Your justice will serve me fine."

"Thank you."

"Please sit down," Dan said to Mana. "We need to go over the details for tomorrow."

Mana agreed, taking a seat at the table. Blue circled around and sniffed the small man. Finding him the right smell he sat on his foot and looked up at him. Mana petted Blue's head and my sense that we could trust him was confirmed.

CHAPTER TWENTY
BAD ASS KITES

The festival was mesmerizing. The sky filled with kites, like hundreds of colorful dots swarming in your vision. When in flight their movements were urgent and lively, but once their string was cut they fell like dead leaves, unhurried and languid, toward the ground. The string, bright pink and dipped in a mixture of glass and rice flour trailed the kite, draping across roofs and people. Perched on the rooftop of an abandoned home that overlooked Shah's buildings, I watched as a green kite drifted toward the ground, its string slicing through the crowd beneath it. Mothers acted quickly to remove it from their children's hair. Friends disentangled it from each other.

And the birds, God, the poor birds. They flew quickly and desperately, weaving between the treacherous string and the flapping kites. They all seemed to make it until one didn't. A fat, grey pigeon, like the ones I grew up with, miscalculated and tangled his delicate wings in the sharp string. He fell to the earth with much more velocity than the lifeless kites.

Thousands of birds died each year during Uttarayan, the Hindu name for the International Kite Festival, which celebrates the end of winter and the approaching harvest season. While traditionally Hindu, the Kite

Festival reaches across religion, class and age groups pulling everyone into it's revelry. Families gather on their roofs to continue long fought, good natured, rivalries with neighbors, cutting each other's kites throughout the day and then trying to outdo each other with fireworks late into the night.

I turned my eyes down to the window of Shah's house and then at my watch. Not even three yet. Since last night an eternity had passed. In the early light of the day Mana had called to tell me Anita was being held in the house, in a guest bedroom. It would take me only about five minutes to reach her from where I sat. Blue waited patiently by my side, curled up in the shade with one eye open and his ears swiveling for sounds, for a signal of some kind.

I pictured Anita tied to a chair, blood running into her eyes. I thought about Dan in the van maneuvering through the city, its streets almost deserted. Everybody was on their roofs. And those who were not engaged with the kites risked their lives. Unsuspecting people died every year from the brightly colored string. It would fall across their paths as they rode on their scooters, jolting them off their mounts and slashing their throats. Amazing to think how much damage a little string could do.

I glanced down into the street below me. A gray cow, chewing on a bright green kite, its mouth dripping a slimy green trail, meandered down the narrow lane. It paused for a moment staring into space, its jaw slack, and then took up its chewing again.

I checked the window again. Checked my watch. Felt cramps in my legs. Stood up and stretched toward my toes making sure to not expose myself to Shah's rooftop fifty yards away. I repeated this routine until it was almost four. Soon they would be getting their tea. Mana said it would take forty-five minutes for the first one to fall.

I peered around the parapet that kept me hidden and stared onto Shah's roof. A young boy ran toward the edge, his little legs unsteady on the pitched roof. His father's arm shot out and brought him back to his mother who picked the boy up. He wriggled, but she clucked at him until the boy rested peacefully in her embrace.

At least forty people spread out over Shah's compound's roofs. There were no railings and the thirty degree tilt of the roof made it look dangerous. But it seemed like everyone was having a good time. Steady on their feet, unafraid of the drop.

Shouts of joy and revelry rose up every time a member of the party managed to cut a kite down. Did they know that there were captors under their feet? That children, used as sex slaves, rested their heads not far away?

I checked my watch again—it was after four. The guards would be drinking their tea. All except the Bulldog, as Mana called him. I hoped he would be too busy to notice a dozen children escaping, Anita's release, and the capture of his boss. Yeah, not likely.

The sun sunk in the sky, bright and burning. I pulled my ball cap lower over my brow and watched the roof. People climbed up and down the wooden ladder, holding cups of chai. The guards must have had theirs. They would be feeling sleepy soon.

I saw Kalpesh climbing the ladder, a sheen of sweat on his brow. He laughed at something and the ladder shook. I felt its wobbles in my gut. This plan needed to work, I did not want to have to chase Kalpesh across these roofs. He'd been playing on them since he was a child and would have an advantage he didn't deserve.

Blue stirred by my side; standing up he stretched out his front paws, raised his head in a massive yawn, and then pushed up against me. I patted him, rubbing under his ears. Blue's eyes rolled back into his skull and one of his back legs thumped rhythmically against the metal roof.

A kite plummeted down and hit the parapet that I crouched behind. A cheer went up, people blew into noise makers, others stomped on the loud roofs. Looking back over, I saw Kalpesh launching a kite. His long kurta was blue silk today, shimmering in the sun. Fingers wrapped in white tape to protect their sensitive skin from the sharp string, Kalpesh flicked his wrist to launch the kite into flight. A young boy stood next to him watching with a slack jaw, holding Kalpesh's spool of string.

I looked at my watch again. It was almost time. Any minute now I'd see Mana climb the ladder and tell Kalpesh to come down to safety, that the guards were passing out. Someone had poisoned them. Dan must be in front of the exit now, the one that the guards were sleeping next to. It was all about to start. My heart beat faster, Blue sensed my excitement and whined softly.

Then I saw Mana's dark head as he climbed the ladder. It hardly jostled under his weight. Kalpesh's attention was on the sky, concentrating on his kite. Mana looked tiny on the roof, his dark suit overly formal and hot compared to the colorful saris and casual jeans of Shah's guests. Kalpesh did not look at Mana when he approached. He was in a hot battle with another kite. I looked up to see the moment that Kalpesh's string was cut. His kite, black with a white crescent moon design, lost its energy and floated, unhindered, toward the ground. Kalpesh turned on Mana with a scowl.

I couldn't hear what either of them said, but Kalpesh's voice was loud and aggressive. His guests glanced over at him nervously. Mana hardly moved until Kalpesh went to push him. Then he simply stepped out of the larger man's way. Kalpesh stumbled forward, but Mana shot out an arm and caught him before he fell. Kalpesh jerked his arm free and, with an outstretched arm, ordered Mana off the roof.

Mana turned back toward the ladder, his face smooth and expressionless. Plan B then, I thought with a sinking stomach. Kalpesh turned to the boy holding his spool of string now limp and kite-less. Shah yelled something, and the boy shoved the spool into the spine of the roof and ran to where the extra kites were kept. A woman dressed in jeans and a lovely bright pink kurta with gold sequin trim chatted with Kalpesh while the boy did his work. Shah's face slowly returned to its regular color as the woman soothed him, at one point even placing her hand on his forearm. He nodded, agreeing with her words.

There was still one bodyguard standing somewhere in the house. I wondered if he would come and get Kalpesh off the roof. The old Bulldog had been with the man for twenty years; he may have more sway than Mana. If all my security started falling asleep I'd cut my party short, but then again I wasn't an egomaniacal pedophile from one of the most powerful families in Gujarat. I didn't actually have parties at all so this line of thinking was getting me nowhere.

I opened the camera app on my phone and flicked through the different angles of the cameras inside the house, looking for the big guy. I saw hallways empty except for slumped security men. The main interior courtyard was filled with guests. They seemed unaware of the shift. I flicked through again, but the Bulldog wasn't visible in any of our cameras. In the nursery the children stood around a sleeping guard.

I felt eyes on me and, looking up, saw a boy about ten or eleven staring down from a flat cement roof. He held two kites, both already with strings. His shirt was worn but clean. I put my finger to my lips and he nodded knowingly. The boy leapt lightly onto the next roof and picked up a fallen kite that hung by its string from the building's gutter. He glanced back at me one more time before disappearing .

All right, I thought. Now or never. Blue and I ducked back into the building. It was old and abandoned, the ceiling caving in and the floors dangerously brittle. I watched where we stepped, tracing our path by the marks we'd left on the dusty ground. Climbing out a window I stretched across a narrow space and scrambled onto one of Kalpesh's balconies. Blue leapt over the open space easily.

We passed a fallen security guard as we made our way through the abandoned halls. Turning back, I patted the guard down. I pulled a small caliber gun out of his shoulder holster and tucked it into the back of my pants. The man breathed heavily, his chin rested on his chest which rose with each inhalation. Mana said it would take six hours for them to wake up. I bet he was going to have one hell of a headache. Blue barked and I whirled around to see a man, dressed in a well-fitted suit, at the end of the hall.

I figured he must be Mugloo, the Bulldog. He was massive, blocking the light from the large window. Shit. Blue's hackles raised as the man approached us. "I think there is something wrong with this man," I said.

The Bulldog didn't answer, he just kept coming toward me, gripping a gun in his left hand. It was very similar to the one I'd just shoved into my pants. Blue's growl rose and he barked again, warning the man off. But this guy was not afraid of Blue. As he got closer I smelled curry-scented body odor. He was broad and bulky, dangerously large. If he hit me even once in the right place I'd be fucked. He stopped ten paces away and smiled. I licked my lips.

"I think he needs medical help," I said, trying to appear the concerned guest. The big guy wasn't buying it. He motioned with his gun for me to come closer. I took a tentative step in his direction. His skin was the color of coconut oil and almost as greasy. Sweat trickled from his hairline. The hallway was hot, the fan above our heads still, the only sound the sleeping man's snores.

"The children are already gone," I lied. He laughed, a soft sound for a man so large. Thrusting his chin in the air he motioned for me to come closer. "Really," I said. "They are gone."

"They don't matter," he said. I felt a chill run down my spine. "We can get more."

I nodded, feeling the truth of his statement. Blue stayed next to me, right behind my right knee as I approached the man. The sound of my steps was softened by a thin rug that ran the length of the hall. I slowed, still out of reach of the loyal bodyguard, whose arms were about twice the length mine. But I must be quicker, I thought. He couldn't be that big and also fast. There was a door to my right, no idea where it led, but maybe I could open it, run inside, shoot him through the door? Didn't sound likely. Looked like I was going to...and then I saw his finger tightening on the trigger. The small opening of the gun was angled right at my gut.

Taking a page from Mana's book I jumped up, kicking off the door, and leapt at the big man's head. He didn't see the move coming and a bullet fired down the hall, thunking into the wall. I landed with both fists coming down hard on his neck, my body slamming into his side. He stumbled away from the blow and bumped into the opposite wall. Recovering quickly he swung his gun arm at me but Blue launched himself, biting down hard and true into the bodyguard's thick forearm.

The gun fell almost soundlessly to the ground. The Bulldog raised his free meaty fist and aimed it at Blue's head. I grabbed onto it. He reversed tactics and smashed his arm, with me attached, into the wall hard enough to rattle my brain. I stayed clamped onto his arm, my vision spotting. He roared as Blue shook his head hard, tearing the man's flesh but not loosening his grip.

The bodyguard slammed me against the wall again. I needed to get to my gun or his. I needed to shoot this giant before he turned my brain to pudding. As I had that thought he threw me off; I fell to the carpeting and rolled out of his reach, pulling the sleeping man's gun from my waist. Looking up I saw the giant holding a new gun pressed to Blue's skull. I was faster. The bullet hit him in the temple and exploded that motherfucker's brains all over the wall. He fell straight down, like a skyscraper during an earthquake. Blue didn't let go of his arm until I called him to my side.

Adrenaline coursed through me. I could feel every muscle in my body, tense and ready, my vision was saturated with colors. I took two deep breaths, smelling the iron scent of blood. Standing over the fallen man I shuddered from the hormones running through me. He almost shot Blue, I thought. And then I shot him again, making his corpse jump and twitch.

The drugged guard continued to slumber as Blue and I walked down the hall. We took a left and I counted off doors until I got to where Mana had said Anita was being held. I knocked on the door, but didn't get an answer. I tried the knob, but found it locked. I put my ear against the door and heard heavy breathing and bodies thrashing.

I got Blue behind me then aimed my gun at the lock and fired. The door exploded splinters and one dug into the back of my hand. It hurt like a bitch. "Shit," I said, as I pulled it out. Blood oozed from the wound.

I pushed on the door, but it still held. Stepping back I kicked at the damaged lock and it popped open. I saw an empty chair; on the table next to it sat a full cup of chai. The noises were louder now, a deep guttural, choking sound. Stepping into the room, my gun extended, Blue behind my right knee, I turned to see a bed, its sheets tangled. Anita stood on it, a man at her knees, and around his neck Anita pulled a chain tight. She was naked, her breasts and biceps vibrating with the effort of choking the man to death. His eyes were bulging, fingers scratching at the metal links tightening around his windpipe. Anita's head was bent over her prey, long, slick black hair covering her face. I watched as the man went limp, the glow in his eyes faded, and then Anita was just tugging on the empty sack of skin left behind by the dead.

"Anita!" I cried out.

Her head jerked up and she stared at me through the curtain of black locks. I recognized the intensity in her eyes. It was the same look I saw in Blue's on that road in Goa. Fear giving way to triumph. Feral.

CHAPTER TWENTY-ONE
SAVING THE CHILDREN

Anita stumbled back. The body slipped onto the bed, but the chain stayed with Anita. It was attached to her wrists, dragging her hands down. "Sydney," she whispered, her voice rough. I ran to the bed and caught her as she fell off the side. Her whole body shook as she sobbed into my arms. With each shudder the chains around her wrists and ankles jangled. I stroked her hair and told her it was over.

"Do you know where the key is?" I asked.

She looked up at me with swollen, red-rimmed eyes. "No," she said.

"We'll find it."

Blue pushed close to Anita, and I went to search the dead man. He still wore his black suit and I found a handcuff key in the inside pocket. I came back around to Anita and unlocked the cuff bracelets on her wrists. She rubbed at the raw skin, as I bent and freed her ankles. "I need clothing," she said. "They cut mine off me."

"Let's take his."

She nodded, but didn't help me as I heaved the body up to remove his jacket. The dead guard was heavy and awkward. I got the jacket off and tossed it on the bed. Unbuttoning his shirt I exposed a broad chest covered in dark hair. I rolled him to get the shirt off and then passed it to Anita. She slipped it over her narrow shoulders, the big white shirt swallowing her small figure.

The pants were already open and pulled down over his hips. I just had to untie and remove the shoes before yanking them off completely. Anita slipped the pants on and tightened the belt, but she still needed to hold them up. I rolled the cuffs for her, being careful not to touch the tender flesh on her ankles. Taking a deep breath I calmed the rage burning inside me at the site of those wounds.

Standing up, I wiped a tear from Anita's cheek. "You did great," I said. "I'm really proud of you."

She nodded, her lips tight.

"Now we've got to get the fuck out of here, are you ready?"

"Yes." I turned to leave, but Anita reached out and pulled on my jacket sleeve. "Are you going to kill Kalpesh?"

I turned back to Anita and her eyes were hard. "I'm going to get him on a plane to France, and justice will be served."

"If you kill him I won't mind."

I smiled. "Good to know. Now let's get the fuck out of this hell hole."

I took her hand and she followed me to the door. With my free hand I pulled my gun and then checked the hallway. It was empty. We rounded the corner and passed by the sleeping guard again. We took a flight of steps down, passed through a long hallway and started up another set of steps. The sound of a woman's laughter filtered down to us. I paused. Anita squeezed my hand, and I heard her breathing turn shallow.

Two pairs of footsteps approached. I looked at the gun in my hand and moments before a couple appeared at the top of the steps, hid it behind my back. But they only had eyes for each other and, upon seeing us, hurried past. The woman's perfume filled my nostrils and its sweetness almost made me gag. I watched them turn the corner and disappear. A part of me wanted to follow them, slam the woman up against the wall, and force her to look at what she did not want to see. But I had more important things to do.

We met no one else on our way to the room where the children were being held. I knocked on the door and Mana opened it. "The Bulldog is dead," I told him.

He nodded, and I walked into the room, still holding Anita's hand. The kids were all scrunched together by the exit holding what few possessions they owned. The room was dirty and shabby, and my heart ached to look at them, so I turned away. Looking up at the sky exposed by the open roof I saw the cheerful kites bobbing high above.

"Thank God," Dan said, as he crossed the room and embraced Anita. She tensed at his touch but then melted into him, grasping at his shirt and burying her head into his chest.

"She was very brave," I told him.

He nodded. "Of course you were," he said to her.

"We must hurry," Mana said.

His arm around Anita, Dan escorted her to the exit. Mana opened the big metal door, its hinges screeching in protest. The blue van waited there. Mana spoke to the children and they followed him obediently outside. I pulled open the side door while Dan helped Anita into the front seat. The van stank of death. As I helped the children in, feeling their soft flesh against my fingers, smelling their youthful scent, seeing the rags that they wore, I wondered what kind of world I was living in and how what I did could possibly be enough. As I helped one boy up, I recognized his big head and realized he was one of the boys I watched enter this place. At least he was safe now, I thought. I would make sure he stayed that way.

Dan came around and touched my elbow. "Hey," he said. I turned to him, feeling tears in my eyes. He smiled. "It's okay."

I shook my head. "It's not," I said. "But you better go. Quickly."

"Mana told me Kalpesh wouldn't come down. You're going after him alone?"

"I'll ask Mana to help but otherwise, yes."

"Let me help."

"No, you've got to get these kids to Chloe and then help Anita to the flight. She can't go alone."

Dan glanced over at Anita who sat in the passenger seat looking so small in the big black suit. He nodded and turned back to me. His arm

159

wrapped around my waist and Dan pulled me close, bringing his head down and pressing his lips to mine. I ran my hands through his hair and down his back, clinging to him, feeling that it may be our last kiss. The taste of tears mingled there in our embrace and then Dan pulled away, his eyes shining.

Without a word he stepped away and climbed into the driver's seat, turning over the engine with a rumble. Mana stood next to me and watched as the van drove down the street and then turned left, disappearing from sight. "Will you help me?" I asked.

Mana put his hand on his younger brother's shoulder, thin and fragile. "I'm sorry, but I must take him to safety."

"You know I may fail without your help."

Mana turned to look at me and I held his gaze. "No, you won't," he said.

Blue and I walked into the interior courtyard on our way to the roof.

The crowd was dense and the people good-looking. As I passed a hush fell on them. They were staring at us, expressions of horror on their plucked and smoothed faces. The gun was still in my hand, loose and ready. Blue was splattered in bright red blood, droplets arched across my shirt. In our wake we left urgent, worried whispers.

We climbed to the top of the steps, and then I paused before ascending the ladder to the roof. I looked up at the people flying kites and laughing. A cheer broke out, and I watched the jubilant celebration with a numb calm. This was only a momentary setback for Shah, I thought. The Bulldog was right. There were more children, a never-ending stream of them. I needed to catch Kalpesh Shah and deliver him to justice or he'd just keep doing what he did. No one would stop him if I didn't.

I tucked my gun into the waist of my jeans and told Blue to wait for me. He can do most things, but climbing a ladder is not one of them. He whined softly as I ascended the ladder; it rattled under me, rushing even more adrenaline into my system. Raising to my full height as I crested the roof line, I saw that the women clustered in the shade were all staring at me, their mouths slightly open with shock.

The sun was sliding down the west side of the world, making the shadows longer and the glow of the kites a little warmer. An excited party on a nearby roof set off a firework that exploded into a thousand golden sparks above us, falling like the branches of a weeping willow. Kalpesh's attention was on his kite. His arms worked in hard jerks as he maneuvered it around another kite's string. With one last pull he was the victor. The cheer was not so loud since half the roof was staring at me and the gun I pointed at Kalpesh.

Shah turned to me, leveling calm eyes on my weapon. "Kalpesh Shah, you need to come with me," I said.

He smiled but I saw sweat spring out in the cleft of his throat. "Don't be ridiculous," he said, glancing around at the crowd. "I'm not going anywhere with you."

"Yes, you are," I said.

Kalpesh's kite, only moments ago victorious, tumbled toward the ground as cheers exploded from another roof and another excited party set off fireworks. The sound ricocheted off the buildings surrounding us, as the bright white globes of fire shot through the air, then faded into the darkening sky.

Kalpesh laughed, a tight sound from his throat. Then he dropped the string from between his fingers and ran across the rooftop. With amazing speed and agility for a man his age, he vaulted over the parapet the ladies were using for shade and leapt onto another roof. I followed in hot pursuit.

The metal roof clanged under our heavy footsteps. The crowd around us stood like still images, their mouths gaping at the spectacle before them. Another firework exploded off a roof sending balls of purple fire flinging through the air.

Kalpesh knew the roofs well. He leapt over a gap and disappeared behind a water tank. I flung myself across the chasm and stumbled onto the ceramic tiles. I landed on my knees hard, but managed to hold onto the gun. My weight broke some of the tiles free, sending them clattering off the edge. I didn't wait to see how long it took for them to hit the pavement below. I scrabbled back to my feet and pushed myself forward.

Rounding the water tower I saw Kalpesh running toward the flat tar roof of an apartment block where another party was going on. Four men stood on the edge, a glowing red Chinese lantern between them. They held it gingerly, waiting until the ghee-fueled flame heated the air inside the balloon enough for it to fly on its own. As Kalpesh grabbed the edge of the roof, hauling himself up, the men let go of the lantern. It struggled for a moment, dipping down. The crowd cried out and then, as it climbed, they cheered. It rose slowly but steadily through the twilight, joining thousands of others all floating toward the horizon.

Kalpesh pulled himself over the roof's edge and then crashed through the party. The crowd of about twenty people yelled and cursed, then swarmed together again, watching his retreating back. I had to stuff the gun back into my pants in order to pull myself up onto the roof. As I stood and pushed my way through, a woman grabbed my arm. I shook her off hard enough that she stumbled. A young man grabbed me then, yelling in Hindi with indignation. With my free hand I pulled out my gun and pointed it at him. His anger turned to fear and his fingers slipped off my arm.

Fireworks were exploding all around us as I pushed through the party. Some of the guests yelled, but the shock of my gun shut them up pretty quick. Reaching the end of the roof I jumped down about five feet onto another metal roof and scanned the rooftops looking for Kalpesh. There were too many parties; he could have slipped into any one of them and disappeared. I bit my lip, thinking hard.

A firework exploded so close I ducked. And then I saw him in its stark light. He was moving quickly from one party to another. I ran across the roof, making a beeline for him. He stopped and waved at me. And then I was falling. My feet broke through the brittle, rusted roof and for a terrifying moment I was dropping through the air as quickly as gravity could take me, an entire portion of the roof coming with me. I put my hands out, dropping the gun, and scrambled to gain a hold on the roof in front of me, the part that wasn't plummeting to earth. My fingers found a grip and I cried out as the metal bit into my hands, the weight of my body pressing them into the jagged edge.

I swung there for a moment looking down at the ancient courtyard below. It was gray with dust and age, the walls crumbled and cracked. The roof lay broken and twisted on the tile floor. Sweat dripped into my eyes. I tried to pull myself up but didn't have a good enough hold. Staring up into the sky I watched the lanterns glide by. I felt my fingers slipping. I cried out in frustration, fear, and futility. I squeezed my eyes shut and gritted my teeth, feeling my fingers slide. Then a strong hand grabbed my wrist and, looking up, I saw Mana above me. I choked on a sob of relief.

He pulled me and I kicked, propelling myself back onto the roof. Mana helped me to my feet. "Quickly," he said. Still holding my hand Mana darted across the roof. My breaths were shallow, but I kept up with him. He lead me off the old metal roof and onto another tile one. "Quickly," he said again. I didn't argue.

Then he crouched low and his eyes narrowed. I followed his gaze and saw Kalpesh on an adjacent roof, laughing and drinking with a group of men, apparently at ease after seeing me fall through the roof. What a stupid, arrogant ass, I thought as I watched one of the men place a firework tube on the edge of the roof and light its fuse. The crowd pushed against the wall of a taller building and with a boom that hurt my ears green spheres of light blasted into the sky.

Mana motioned for me to go in one direction while he set off in the other. It wasn't until I was almost in front of Kalpesh that he saw me. His eyes opened in shock. Dropping his glass, he turned. But he only got two steps before running into Mana, who took him out at the knees, sending him crashing onto his face. I leapt past the stunned crowd and straddled Shah, yanking back one arm and then the other. Forcing his wrists together I held them tight against his back. He yelled in pain. Pulling a zip tie out of my back pocket, I looped it around his wrists and tightened it so that his skin bulged.

Mana helped me lift him off the ground. "Help me!" Kalpesh yelled at the crowd. They stared back with wide and frightened eyes, no one making a move. Holding Kalpesh's elbow I moved him toward the lip of the roof, back towards his house. Mana helped me get him across the broken metal roof and then showed me a shortcut back to Kalpesh's house. The whole time Shah hollered for help, but the boom of fireworks and the indifference of his neighbors left him firmly in my grasp.

Kalpesh's roof was deserted, littered with broken kites and crisscrossed with bright pink string. The beautiful people had beaten a hasty retreat, apparently indifferent to their host's fate. Kalpesh tried to yank away from me. I punched him hard in the gut. He doubled over, his breath leaving him in a whoosh. "Why?" he wheezed. "Who are you?"

I didn't answer. Instead I pulled him forward, thinking about our next step. I had the keys to one of Kalpesh's cars and Mana and I just needed to get him into the trunk, then drive to the airport...

"What am I to you?" he yelled, his voice cracking.

"Shut the fuck up," I said.

Above us two lanterns collided, bursting into flame and plummeting toward the roof in a plume of jet black smoke. I dodged to avoid the fireball and Kalpesh wrenched free, taking off back the way we'd come. He stumbled on a kite spool sticking out from the roof's spine. For a moment I thought he would regain his balance, but with his hands locked behind him he couldn't. His body rolled down the pitched roof gaining speed as it reached the edge. The string wrapped around him as he spun. Mana and I raced toward him but Kalpesh fell, a cry of terror escaping him as he hit the open air. The string tangled around his body snapped piece by piece, jerking him with each break. Kalpesh glanced off the bougainvillea clinging to the boundary wall and then smashed onto the ground. Wrapped in kite string, his legs at odd angles and neck at an unnatural tilt, a pool of blood spreading around him, Kalpesh Shah lay dead in the courtyard of his ancestral home. Several kites and a handful of bright pink petals he'd shaken loose from the bougainvillea floated down to join him.

CHAPTER TWENTY-TWO
CHANGE OF PLANS

Mana looked over at me and then turned and bolted across the roof toward the ladder. I followed him. Blue barked when he saw me. He spun in tight circles as I descended from the roof. Mana was already gone. I raced down the steps, past sleeping security guards, and out the front door. Blue paused for a moment to sniff Shah's body, but I brushed past it and pulled open the compound's gate, entering the street. Blue jogged to keep up with me as I hurried down the alley, keeping one eye on the lanterns that floated above my head.

Fireworks continued to explode and light up the night sky as I headed back toward Anita's place. I unlocked the door and before pushing it open I looked around. The lane was empty. Stepping into the old house I closed the heavy doors behind me and shut my eyes, releasing a breath. I stood there in the darkness for a moment sucking in air. Fuck. That was not what was supposed to happen.

I made my way up to our room and sat on the bed, resting my head in my hands. Blue sat next to me, scooting close, placing his head on my knee with a sigh. My phone chirped and I answered. "Dan," I said. "Kalpesh is dead."

"Where are you?"

"I'm safe. You need to take off, get Anita to Paris."

"What?"

"Just go."

"Aren't you coming?"

"Not now."

"Will you meet me back in Goa?"

"I'm not sure." I paused. "I need some time to think."

"Think?"

"About your idea, about..." I didn't know what to say. There was something holding me here for the moment. I couldn't imagine going to the airport, boarding a plane, and leaving this place.

"Really? About Joyful Justice?" he said, a note of excitement in his voice.

"Don't call it that. I just need to think. Don't get so excited."

"I'm not getting too excited," he said, but I could almost see the grin on his face.

I cringed. "Just..." I let my sentence end there and sighed.

"Where are you going to go?" Dan asked.

"I'm not sure. I'll call you. Be safe."

"You too, Captain."

I hung up and stared at the window. The wind blew the curtains, white against a sky filled with red, green, and yellow lanterns. The flash of a firework silhouetted Mana in the window, crouched like a bird on the edge of the sill. I gasped at his sudden appearance.

"You are a brave warrior," he said in his soft voice.

I laughed. "Funny you should say that since you just scared the shit out of me."

He laughed softly, his voice floating on the same wind that billowed the curtains around him. "Come in," I said.

He shook his head. "No time. Just wanted to say thank you."

"I'm the one who should say thank you," I said. "You saved my life tonight."

He nodded. I thought he'd disappear again, but instead he bowed his head and mumbled in a language I did not understand. Raising his voice he said, "Do not lose your way, only the path of the brave will suit you."

I opened my mouth to speak but he leaned back and was gone. I ran to the window just in time to see him swing to the street and flee into the shadows. Watching the empty alley I felt the breeze on my face and breathed in the night air. It smelled of sulfur and smoke, acrid and heavy.

I crossed the room and looked out across the roofs toward Shah's place, wondering what was going on over there. Were the police there? I opened the window and leaned on the edge, watching the parties of people spread over the roofs, setting off fireworks, reveling in the danger and brilliance of the flying flames.

I hooked a leg over the sill and climbed out onto the roof. Blue jumped his front paws on the ledge, and I motioned for him to join me. I crouched, resting on my heels and wished that Kalpesh hadn't fallen, that I'd done what I wanted to do. Now he was just another corpse; another death on my soul when he could have been so much more.

Blue sat close to me, and I wrapped my arm across his shoulders. He leaned into me and I almost fell over, putting out my free hand to balance. "You still love me, huh, boy?" He licked at my ear in response and I laughed, dodging his tongue.

At least the kids were safe with Agapito. They had a chance, I thought. Chloe and Agapito were good people. I wondered what they'd think when news of Kalpesh's demise reached them. Would they know I tried? Or think that I'd bound a man and tossed him to his death? Maybe they'd know I wouldn't have bothered with the binding if I planned on killing him. It didn't matter. What people thought of me wouldn't change anything. Nothing could bring Kalpesh back, take away those kids' trauma, or allow justice to take its course. It was over and it turned out how it did. The question was: Where to next?

My phone rang and I climbed back inside, picking it up off the bed. Checking the screen I saw it was Darcy, my contact at the jet share company I had hired for the flight to Paris. "I just spoke with Dan," she said. "You didn't leave?"

"No, I'm still here."

"Do you need me to arrange alternative transportation?"

I walked over to the window and looked back toward Kalpesh's. A blue firework exploded and I thought for a second it was the reflection of a police cruiser's light, come to investigate Shah's death. "Yes," I said. "I'd like to leave Ahmedabad tomorrow morning."

I heard the clicking of her nails against a keyboard. "We have a lot of planes available."

I pictured flying above the city, leaving it all behind and I didn't think I was ready to go so high, so far, so fast. Nor did it seem wise to show my passport at an airport, given how many people witnessed those rooftop escapades. "I'd prefer a car."

The typing stopped. "Okay, where do you want to go?"

I shook my head, watching a lantern's slow progress as its flame burned out and the red paper dome headed toward the roof. "I'm not sure. Where would you recommend?"

The typing started again as the last flicker of light died in the paper lantern and it swung side-to-side picking up speed. Blue barked as it approached, moving toward us quickly. "What about Udaipur, it's about three or four hours north. Supposed to be a really phenomenally beautiful city."

The lantern bumped into the roof and slid down the incline, rolling, tumbling, crumpling as it went. "Is it in Gujarat?"

"No, Rajasthan."

"Sounds perfect," I said, as the lantern tipped off the edge and disappeared.

"We have a relationship with a hotel there."

"Fine," I said.

"How long do you plan to stay?"

"Not sure."

"I'll book it for three nights and we can always extend."

"Great," I said, feeling suddenly tired and ready for bed. Patting my palm against my thigh brought Blue back inside and, gripping the phone between my shoulder and cheek, I closed the window, pulling the curtains shut.

"Where do you want the car to pick you up?" Darcy asked. I gave her the name of a nearby hotel. "The car will be there at nine a.m.," she said. "Is there anything else I can do for you?"

"No, thanks for calling, Darcy."

She cleared her throat. "There is one more thing."

"Yes?"

"Mulberry called me looking for you," she continued quickly. "Of course, I didn't give him any information but, he asked that you call him."

"Thanks, Darcy. Have a good night."

I hung up the phone and sat on the bed, staring at it for a moment. I scrolled to Mulberry's number. My finger hovered over his name. But I clicked the phone off, not ready to talk to him or anyone else that night.

Looking around the room I realized I didn't have any clothing, that all my luggage was on its way to Paris with Anita and Dan. The clothing I wore was filthy and I peeled it off, heading down the steps, naked, for a bath.

The crack of fireworks sounded like a dull thud in the bathroom. I filled a copper bucket from a tap at knee height in the wall, then pulled over the small wooden stool and sat. The water was boiling and I added some cold before filling a mug and pouring it over my head. The yellow tiles, with small blue flowers curling across them, dewed in the closed space.

I used a bar of soap on my hair and my body, enjoying the rich fragrance that the suds released. My feet left dark, dirty prints. I rubbed them clean, pouring more mugs over my body to keep from feeling a chill. Clean and tired I wrapped myself in a towel and walked into Anita's room.

Her desk was bare, the bed neatly made. I wondered if she'd come back. And if she did, what would she do? Could she return to reporting after all we'd done? Opening her closet I found a few sundresses hanging there. Pulling them off the hangers I took them with me upstairs.

I draped the towel over a chair before climbing between the sheets. My wet hair tickled my face, and I pulled it up and away. Sleep would not come.

Mana's words taunted me as I watched the ceiling fan spin and shake. What should I do? The path of the brave? What did he mean? It felt like a challenge. Like a call to action, but maybe that was just Dan's influence.

I'd thought maybe working again would help, but I was still left with an emptiness. Why couldn't I just love him and we could work on cases together for the rest of our lives? Couldn't we be really good together?

I rolled onto my side and thought about Dan, picturing him smiling down at me, his hair flopping onto his brow, his grape-green eyes glittering. He was cute, fun, loyal, smart, good, solid, trustworthy. Everything that you would look for in a partner. He even challenged me to do more and be better. We'd only had one fight. What was wrong with me, I marveled, that I didn't want to be with him? What was wrong with me that I didn't want a ring on my finger? To be bound to someone. To have a partner.

I rolled onto my back and stared up at the fan again. Maybe it was because I didn't believe that Dan understood how fucked up I was. He did not understand what drove me forward. The man thought I believed most people were good and was fighting for some kind of balance. But really it's just some kind of sick urge that drives me forward. It's like a high almost. Doing good by doing bad. It's what I crave.

Or maybe it was Mulberry's kiss. The thought popped into my head unwanted, unwarranted, and without warning. I rolled onto my side and stared at the wall, trying to clear my mind by counting, but I could almost hear Mulberry laughing. I felt heat in my cheeks and rolled again, twisting the sheets around my legs, tying myself up. There were so many things wrong with him and me. I didn't trust him. Oh, I trusted him with my life but he always thought he knew what was best for me. The man didn't have faith in my ability to take care of myself.

But...I shook my head, trying again to clear it of any thoughts, but it didn't work. I sat up. Blue raised his head, his collar jingling. Flopping back onto the bed I counted the ceiling fans rotations until I fell asleep.

I dreamt of a desert that never ended. I walked through it, the heat like a heavy blanket. Where was Blue? I wondered, right before I started sinking into the loose sand. I woke up choking.

CHAPTER TWENTY-THREE
MOURNING

The next day I left for Udaipur, an ancient city to the north. I fell asleep during the car ride, unburdened of all responsibility but Blue. I was loose again. I'd felt pure tension for the last couple of weeks, my mind always churning, my body coiled and ready to attack. Now that it was over, my head lolled on the doily-draped seat back.

There was still plastic on all the handles and knobs, trying to keep the cab clean and new looking. The driver had eyed Blue nervously, but he'd agreed on a price and that price included a dog. Darcy had just failed to mention how big the dog was. He didn't look afraid at least, just wary of his seat cushions.

The drive was about four hours, and I was awake only until we left the city. It was right as we entered the desert that I drifted off. Its bleak emptiness let the waves jumping in my brain settle down.

I slept heavily, awakening only when Blue's wet nose nudged at my cheek moments before a uniformed bellboy opened my door. I was swept up into luxury, into the penthouse suite. It was gorgeous. I stood out on the marble balcony and I could see the lake and the white marble palace at its sparkling center.

I wondered at a world where there were so few on top and so many on the bottom. Is that human nature? That we are not equal? That there are those who are born with the right, the passion, the luck, the forbear-ance, the whatever it takes to get them to the top and then there are those who are not? Is the too-familiar dynamic of oppressed and oppressor the natural order of things? Or has that order been trans-muted, destroyed, in some way corrupted by the human mind?

Carrying my melancholy thoughts to the lobby, I spoke with a woman behind the front desk about professional mourners. She was young and eager to please. Her uniform was a pattern of greens, like the jungle looks in kids' books; bright and airy, not dense and moist.

With a nervous smile the clerk sent me over to the concierge, a man with a chicken neck, Gandhi glasses, a white collared shirt, vest, tie, but no jacket. If he'd worn black bands on his arms and a green visor he would have looked like an old- fashioned bank teller. The man sat at a large wooden desk in a discrete corner of the lobby, waiting for the chance to be useful.

I sat across from him in a wooden chair, its seat, back, and arms upholstered in burgundy leather, like a poodle. Blue sat next to me, his vision gliding over the top of the desk. To our left the receptionist checked in a family of Swedes, two tall, elegant parents and three chubby blonde kids that reminded me of beach balls with heads, legs, and arms. Maybe it was something about the striped shirts they wore.

To our right the hotel bar had an aristocratic air—paisley carpeting, long thick drapes, mahogany paneling, and deep couches. A woman leaned on the bar, a little too drunk, a little too old, clutching a small white dog so tightly that it choked.

"My brother was murdered," I told the man.

He made a small gasp and reached out for a pen on his desk as though notes might be necessary with such a claim.

"I want to hire mourners."

The man leaned closer and asked in a polite and crisp accent that I repeat myself. "I want to hire professional mourners, you know, the women who cry at funerals," I said.

"Ah, yes," he said quietly. "I see." But I didn't think he did because he just looked confused. Why would a western woman want mourners for her brother?

"He was murdered here?" the man asked, his mouth a thin line of regret.

"No..." I faltered, unwilling or unable to put my reasons into words.

Seeing my hesitation he jumped in; after all it was his job to take care of anyone who sat across from him. Assuming, of course, that they were staying in the hotel.

"How many would you like to hire?"

"How many does one usually get?"

He leaned back in his chair and pursed his lips. "It depends on the family's wealth, the importance of the individual," he said quietly.

"What is the most that any funeral has ever had?"

"I'm not sure," he admitted. "I'd be happy to find out for you."

I sat back in my chair and thought about it. Now I was suddenly trying to figure out how many mourners it would take to soak away my grief.

"One hundred sounds like it might do," I said.

"Madame, there are not even a hundred mourners left in the city. It is a dying tradition."

"Dying," I repeated to myself.

"Perhaps I could get ten, maybe fifteen."

"Where would they do it?"

"Where?"

"Yes, where would they mourn?"

"Wherever you told them, Madame."

I nodded. "Okay. I'm going out now. See how many you can get and I'll let you know where I want them."

"Yes, Madame."

I stood up, then turned back to the man. "Is there a shop in the hotel?"

He nodded and directed me deeper into the lobby. I followed the marble hall to a store that sold exactly what I needed. Decked out in my new running shorts and T-shirt, a brand new phone clenched in my fist, and Blue by my side, I headed out for a run.

The streets were crowded and loud. There were no sidewalks, and I kept getting stopped by passing traffic. I shook my head trying to clear it. Trying to step into the flow rather than be stopped by it. I approached a large temple with tall, narrow steps that led up to the entrance. I paused at the bottom of the stairs and watched people pouring in and out of the sacred building, white against a bright blue sky. An old, toothless woman wearing a bright red sari held wrinkled hands up to her pathetic mouth and cried at me. I shook my head at the beggar and turned, running past the intricately carved temple built for the gods that had forsaken her.

I turned up the volume on my headphones, drowning out the honking and talking. The only sound I could hear was the steady electronic beat of Miike Snow's *Animal*.

When sweat covered my body and the thick smell of smoke and spices became too much for me, I headed back to the hotel. As I pushed past a group of men arguing about a turned over cart, its melons spread across the road being squished by cars and carried away by monkeys, I looked up at the mountains that ringed the city and something in their steadiness stopped me in the middle of all that chaos. The perfect reminder of how small and fleeting we humans are.

Upon my reentering my hotel lobby the concierge rose from his chair and approached me. I smiled at him. Gently taking my elbow he led me over to his desk. Settled back in my chair I told him I wanted the mourners to start at the temple and then come right under my balcony.

"Yes, Madame. It will be so."

CHAPTER TWENTY-FOUR
CLUTCHING, FIGHTING, DYING FOR YOU

The wailing outside filled me with its sound and I felt grief coursing through every fiber of my being. It felt cleansing, to revel in the pain, stop trying to push it down where it couldn't touch me. It was what had created me, I realized, as sobs racked through me. This pain, the loss of my brother, of my identity, it was something to be reveled in, not scorned and pushed aside.

I let screams of grief escape me, adding to the cacophony that rose from the women clustered in the street below. I was an animal, nothing more and nothing less. Blue barked and then raising his nose to the sky let out a howl that warbled in his throat.

I didn't hear the knocking at the door, but suddenly Mulberry was at my side. He picked me up off the ground. "Sydney," he said, shaking me. "Sydney. Joy!"

He looked down at me with his bright green eyes and I grabbed onto him, clawing at his back, pulling him closer to me. Then he was kissing me and I was kissing him. We stumbled back into the suite and knocked into a table, sending a lamp crashing to the ground. He pushed me onto the table, kissing me, his hands rough. I felt on fire and wild. I pushed him back, slamming him into a nearby wall sending a photograph smashing to the ground, its frame cracked and the glass shattered, sending splinters across the marble floor.

Blue barked and circled us. Mulberry growled, then picked me up and carried me past the destruction. I fought against him, pounding on his chest. He let me hit him, hardly feeling it. He was so much stronger, braver, bigger, more than me. I cried out again and he silenced me with his mouth.

Slamming the bedroom door behind us with his foot he dropped me on the bed. He threw off his shirt. On my knees, I pulled my dress over my head. He grabbed me and I tore at his hair as he kissed me. We fought, pillows flying off the bed, sheets tangling and catching us, but he didn't let me go.

The wailing outside continued, but now sounded distant compared to the rapid beating of my heart and ragged breaths I managed to pull. He pinned me under him, sweat slick between us. I dug my nails into his back so that he winced. He bit me hard.

I bucked my hips, tumbling us together across the bed and onto the floor, landing with him under me. He reached up and held my face, looking up at me, his eyes shining. I bit my lip, looking down at him, my chest heaving. He sat up and gently kissed my clavicle, trailing to my shoulder. Mulberry ran his hands up my back slowly, caressing me. I twitched when he touched the scar on my leg. "Shhh," he said into my neck. I leaned my head back staring up at the ceiling and let myself float away with him.

We exhausted ourselves, and I fell asleep against his chest. Mulberry ran his fingers lightly up and down my arm, soothing me into a dream-less blackness. I woke up sweating and tangled in the sheets. Mulberry twitched in his sleep and cried out. "Wake up," I said, shaking him. He struggled for a moment and then his eyes popped open, wide and terri-fied. "It was just a dream," I said. "Hey," I smiled. "It was just a dream."

His eyes focused on me. He shook his head. "Then what are you doing in bed with me?"

I laughed. "Did you seriously just say that?"

His arm wrapped around me and this time was slow, gentle. I saw scars on his body I'd never noticed before. A slash across his left bicep, the puckered kiss of a bullet exit wound on his right thigh. A zigzag across his abdomen looked fresh, new, still healing.

When I woke up, the morning light poured through the floor to ceiling windows and I was alone in bed. Scanning the room I saw destruction. A side table was turned over, the lamp askew on the ground. The sheets were ripped off the mattress and tangled around my body. The memories from the night before rushed back at me, hot and heavy in the morning light. I touched my lips, swollen. I walked naked to the bathroom and took a hot shower, finding a bruise on my hip, a bite mark on my neck, and finger marks on my bicep.

Wiping steam off the mirror I saw me staring back, my cheeks flushed, lips plump. I ran a comb through my hair, pulling at the tangles. Taking a moment I made eye contact with myself in the mirror and felt a sense of peace I hadn't felt in years. I couldn't help but smile.

Pulling on one of the big, white, fluffy bathrobes provided by the hotel I walked out into the living room. The mess was worse. Glass scattered across the floor caught the morning light reflecting my true nature back at me. Dangerous animal, I thought.

"Hey," Mulberry said. He was standing on the balcony wearing the other robe. His brown hair with specks of grey was tousled and his smile unsure.

"Hi," I said back, picking my way through the glass toward him. We didn't know what to do. I stood in front of him and the way he looked down at me made my body hum, but he ran his hand through his hair, something it looked like he'd been doing all morning and said:

"There's something I need to tell you." He looked at the table where a pot of coffee and two cups waited. "You want some coffee?"

"Sure," I said. He pulled my chair out for me, and I laughed at him.

He blushed. "Sorry," he said, leaving me to my own devices to pour my coffee. Mulberry sat across from me and picked up his own cup taking a sip. "I'm sure you're wondering what I'm doing here."

It hadn't even occurred to me why Mulberry was there. He just always showed up when I needed him. The thought struck me silent and Mulberry continued fiddling with his coffee cup. "Hugh is in trouble."

His words were like a splash of frigid water. "What?" I croaked. Hugh was James's boyfriend when he was murdered. At the time I thought that Hugh would be my brother-in-law soon enough. I knew he mourned James almost as much as me. I'd promised to call him after I fled New York, to let him know I was safe, but I never did hoping to keep all those feelings far away.

Mulberry looked at me. "He's been accused of murder."

"Murder?" The idea seemed absurd. Hugh was gentle, sweet. Then again, I don't think anyone would have pegged me for a killer before I became one.

"We've got him a lawyer and he's already out on bail, but I thought you'd want to come help."

I nodded. "Yes, of course." Sipping my coffee I looked out onto the lake sparkling serenely in the early light. "Wait a second," I said, turning back to Mulberry. "Who's we?"

His cheeks flushed. "Someone you don't like very much."

"Jesus, Mulberry, Bobby Maxim!"

"Hey, he's the one who brought this to my attention."

"Why are you still in contact with that guy?"

"He's not all bad."

"He tried to have us killed!"

Mulberry rubbed at the stubble on his face. "I don't hold that against him."

I slammed my coffee down, rattling the saucer.

"Look," Mulberry leaned toward me. "He's willing to help, and we're going to need as much as we can get. Hugh is in deep shit here."

I squeezed my eyes shut and pressed my palms against my sockets. My phone buzzed. Mulberry got up and grabbed my purse for me. I pulled my phone out and saw that I'd missed Dan's call...seven times. I hung my head, guilt coursing through my body.

The phone rang again as I held it, a number I didn't recognize. I answered. "Hello, Sydney." His voice sent a shiver down my spine.

"Bobby?"

"I guess Mulberry has told you about Hugh by now."

"Yes."

"Your flight leaves in two hours. I'm sure Hugh will be very excited to see you." I didn't answer, feeling like the world was tipping on its side. "I bet you're going to look real good in Miami. See you soon, dear."

The line went dead.

EK

Turn the page to read an excerpt from
The Devil's Breath, Sydney Rye Mysteries Book 5, or purchase it now and continue reading Sydney's next adventure:
emilykimelman.com/DB

EK

Sign up for my newsletter and stay up to date on new releases, free books, and giveaways:
emilykimelman.com/News

SNEAK PEEK

THE DEVIL'S BREATH, SYDNEY RYE MYSTERIES
BOOK 5

LONG DAY'S JOURNEY INTO NIGHT

At the end of a long journey, lightning flashed outside my window...*I need more control.*

My hand jumped to Mulberry's forearm and squeezed. Shutting my eyes I struggled not to picture the small plane cracking in half, my body flying through the air, still seat belted to the beige leather chair; Blue, his paws grasping at empty space, disappearing into the bruise colored clouds.

The small jet shook and our pilot's voice, smooth and steady, came over the loudspeaker, "Sorry about the bumps, we'll have you down in Miami in about twenty minutes. Just hold tight."

Mulberry put his hand over mine. "Don't worry," he said. "We'll be there soon."

He smiled, making his crow's feet crinkle. Mulberry's eyes were deep emerald with ochre and flashes of gold. I tried to smile back but could tell I was just giving a grimace. Mulberry handed me his whiskey and soda. I finished it off.

The ice cubes danced in my empty glass. Then we were suddenly out of the clouds. Below us the ocean was close, steel blue with white caps cresting each wave. The city's skyscrapers looked like towers of mercury in the storm's eerie light. Rain drops clung to my window, streaking across it as our speed pushed them aside.

Hugh was somewhere down there in that city, a flat landscape made multi-dimensional through the efforts of man. My stomach lurched as we dropped through the air, my seat belt pressing against my stomach. Blue whined softly and flattened himself even further onto the floor of the plane.

A giant of a dog, Blue has the coat of a wolf, the snout of a Collie, with one brown eye and one blue. Both of which were trained on me at that moment. My fear was freaking him out. Closing my eyes I tried to imagine the turbulence as a gentle rocking but it didn't work. An ice cube jumped out of my glass landing on the carpeting. Blue, his belly still flat on the ground, inched his way toward it, then his tongue stretched out and pulled the cube into his mouth. He crunched twice before looking back up at me, now hoping for more whiskey- flavored ice. I couldn't help but smile at the expectant look on his fuzzy face.

We touched down with a jerk that sent my heart racing one more time. But as we slowly taxied toward our hangar the storm seemed suddenly minor. Just a breath of wind fluttered across the puddles, turning them into shimmering mirrors framed by the dark tarmac.

"All right Ms. Rye," our captain's voice came back on over the loud-speaker. "Sorry about that descent but we got you here safe. Thanks for flying with us, I hope we'll have you back real soon."

As soon as humanly possible I thought to myself. I didn't want to be here, but Hugh was in trouble and if there was one person I cared about in this world it was him. He was a tie to my murdered brother, a shared memory bank. I wondered what his reaction would be when he saw me. The world thought I was dead. Somehow I felt that Hugh would know I wasn't. It was possible, I recognized, that the guilt of not letting him know I was alive gave me unrealistic hopes.

Robert Maxim was waiting in the hangar. I stopped at the top of the steps and looked down at him. He smiled, his eyes brightening. Maxim was taller than Mulberry but not as broad, more lean and fluid. Robert's rich brown hair was turning a brilliant silver at the temples. "You're looking a little green," he said as I made my way down the steps, his hazel eyes picking up the blue in his tie and twinkling at me. Like we were friends. Like he never tried to kill me.

"And you're looking a little orange," I answered, referring to the man's tan.

He laughed deeply, the sound bouncing around in the large hangar. Behind Robert, a tall man dressed in a dark suit and wearing a driver's cap stood in front of a sleek black limo. Robert turned to him. "Claude," he waved the man over. Claude looked like a Claude, like a character from a kickboxing movie. The one with the scar across his chest and mammoth reach. But, who, of course, is bested by our plucky hero, or heroine as the case may be. "He can take your luggage," Robert said.

I held up my small duffel. "This is all I've got."

Robert raised an eyebrow. "I love a woman who travels light."

"Bobby," Mulberry said, reaching out his hand.

Maxim took it and shook, smiling. "You got our girl back," he said to Mulberry.

I bristled but bit my tongue. Without Maxim's intervention I wouldn't know Hugh was in trouble. But that didn't mean I was their "girl" or that I was "back".

Claude took my bag and opened the door for me. I climbed in, scooting to the far bench so that my back was against the driver's seat. Blue followed me, turning so that he could settle his side against my legs and face the door. Mulberry came next, his broad shoulders making it hard for him to maneuver in the narrow space. I flashed back to last night, his thick arms and rough hands holding my hips, and felt a blush creep up my neck. He smiled as he sat on the bench to my left, which faced the bar. I turned to the row of liquor bottles, busying myself making another whiskey and soda. Bobby sat closest to the door facing me across the long expanse of space.

A fresh drink in my hand I sat back into the soft black leather as the car rolled out of the private airport. "Does Hugh know I'm alive?" I asked.

Bobby shrugged. "I didn't tell him."

"Where is he?"

"At his apartment. We can go there now if you want."

"Yes," I said and then turned away from him, looking through the tinted windows. Puddles swelled around sewer drains. As we passed through them, our car pushed waves onto the sidewalks as high as people's calfs. Pedestrians hurried through the mess, raising their knees high and clutching umbrellas with white knuckles.

We stopped at a light and I watched a man standing on the corner, his face tilted toward the receding clouds, arms loose at his sides, ignoring the foaming gray-green water that swirled around his ankles.

As crazy as mo...

Continue reading *The Devil's Breath*: emilykimelman.com/DB

AUTHOR'S NOTE

Thank you for reading my novel, *Strings of Glass*. I'm excited that you made it here to my "note". I'm guessing that means that you enjoyed my book. If so, would you please write a review for *Strings of Glass*? You have no idea how much it warms my heart to get a new review. And this isn't just for me, mind you. Think of all the people out there who need reviews to make decisions. The children who need to be told this book is not for them. And the people about to go away on vacation who could have so much fun reading this on the plane. Consider it an act of kindness to me, to the children, to humanity.

Let people know what you thought about *Strings of Glass* on your favorite ebook retailer.

Thank you,

Emily

ACKNOWLEDGMENTS

This book would not exist without the help of a lot of people.

I'd like to start with the Lakhias. They were the most gracious and warm hosts while I was in India. They opened their homes to me and made me feel very welcome. Thank you from the bottom of my heart.

My best friend, Mette, is the most patient, eloquent, and encouraging of coaches, helping me find the story amongst my jumbles of words. Without her insights this book would not be the same.

Families that support you in the wildest of your dreams are not easy to find but I was lucky enough to grow up in one. Thank you Nana, Ma, Da, David and Sam.

ABOUT THE AUTHOR

I write because I love to read...but I have specific tastes. I love to spend time in fictional worlds where justice is exacted with a vengeance. Give me raw stories with a protagonist who feels like a friend, heroic pets, plots that come together with a BANG, and long series so the adventure can continue. If you got this far in my book then I'm assuming you feel the same...

Sign up for my newsletter and
never miss a new release or sale:
emilykimelman.com/News

I also have an exclusive Facebook group just for my readers! Join *Emily Kimelman's Insatiable Readers* to stay up to date on sales and releases, have exclusive giveaways, and hang out with your fellow book addicts: emilykimelman.com/EKIR.

If you've read my work and want to get in touch please do! I loves hearing from readers.
www.emilykimelman.com
emily@emilykimelman.com

facebook.com/EmilyKimelman
instagram.com/emilykimelman

EMILY'S BOOKSHELF

Visit www.emilykimelman.com to purchase your next adventure.

EMILY KIMELMAN
MYSTERIES & THRILLERS

Sydney Rye Mysteries

Unleashed

Death in the Dark

Insatiable

Strings of Glass

Devil's Breath

Inviting Fire

Shadow Harvest

Girl with the Gun

In Sheep's Clothing

Flock of Wolves

Betray the Lie

Savage Grace

Blind Vigilance

Fatal Breach

Undefeated

Coming Fall 2022

Starstruck Thrillers

A Spy Is Born

EMILY REED

URBAN FANTASY

Kiss Chronicles

Lost Secret

Dark Secret

Stolen Secret

Buried Secret

Coming Late 2022

Lost Wolf Legends

Butterfly Bones

Coming Summer 2022

Made in the USA
Middletown, DE
22 August 2022

71784021R00118